MOUNTAIN INK

SAPPHIRE LAKE

DARLENE TALLMAN

CONTENTS

COPYRIGHT

BLURB

After nearly one thousand years under water thanks to Tamsin's curse, Dax Carlson feels he will never find his mate. Each month, it gets more and more difficult to return to the surface for the three days he's allowed. But he's not quite ready to throw in the proverbial towel and instead, decides that he will finally get the tattoo he's been plotting with the new owner of Mountain Ink, Jesse Halstead.

Racine Halstead is in over her head and she knows it, having promised her uncle that she would run his tattoo shop while he sees to his father's estate. A native of Aurora Falls, she's aware of the legend as she also does caretaking duties at several of the monthly visitors' cabins. She just never expects that one will come in wanting a tattoo or that he'll wind up being her mate.

Suitable for ages 18+ due to adult themes and language, as well as a sexy merman!

ACKNOWLEDGMENTS

I want to say thank you to Moxie North and P Jameson for inviting me into their world. Having read the other stories, I was captivated and when the call was put out for a few more authors, I raised my hand and was accepted! I've had a blast writing it and hope that it does the series justice. I also want to thank Meester PJ of AgentX Graphics who created the gorgeous covers for this amazing series!

DEDICATION

For my oldest son, Tony, and his beautiful wife, my daughter-in-love, Dani, whose birthdays are on December 7th, one year apart from each other. I'm so proud of the life you two have built and the grandkids you've blessed me with, even if I don't see y'all as much as I want. May you both always chase your dreams and teach the kids that the world is theirs for the taking!

PROLOGUE

A love so true, the earth rejoiced.

A betrayal so cruel, the stars cried.

Those that chose to ignore my pain,

Will forever be bound to the earth they

Tried to steal. My heart is black to their

Cries of pain. Your souls will twist in

The mud below just as the fish dig for food.

You'll suffer as I have under each full moon.

Until such time that you find your true love.

CHAPTER 1
PRESENT DAY

Racine

"Are you sure about this, Uncle Jesse?" I ask, as we sit in his office at Mountain Ink. Aurora Falls may be a small community, and there's already one tattoo shop, but we're located on the other side of town. Uncle Jesse said that since we had so many tourists, there was enough business to go around.

"Honey, you know everything I do and I'm more than confident that you can handle anything that comes up while I'm gone," he replies, shuffling through some papers on his desk. "Now, I need you to sign this so you can handle the banking while I'm gone." I look down at the form from the bank that adds me to the accounts as a verified signatory or some shit. Raising panicked eyes in his direction, I point to the form.

"What does this mean?"

"That you can handle anything at the bank as if you were me," he states. "Raci, you can do it." I shrug because my self-confidence has never been all that great, thanks to a shitty upbringing. If not for Uncle Jesse and Aunt Carla, I would probably be dead or in jail. Instead, they stepped in and brought me under their roof, then spent the last ten years pouring good into my life. I still falter when it comes to some things, though, and handling important shit like the shop's bank account is one of them.

"If you think so. I still can't believe that Grandpa Paul didn't want a big service," I reply.

"He wanted everyone to remember him how he was, not how he ended up being when he passed," he tells me. I nod because by the time he found out he had cancer, he was riddled with it and ended up being a shell of his former self, according to Aunt Carla.

"Are you sure your customers will be okay with me working on them?" I've been apprenticing with him since I was sixteen, and about three years ago, I started inking the walk-in clients. I've built up a customer base of my own, but with Uncle Jesse leaving for a bit, I may have to step in on a few of his and that makes me nervous as hell.

"If they're not, they'll have to wait for me to come back," he replies. "Now, I've done the inventory order, but I want to show you how it's done in case you run low on anything."

I shake my head at all the information he's already tossed at me. "Please tell me it's not a handwritten thing, Uncle Jesse."

"Nope, your aunt got me into the twenty-first century," he says, opening up the laptop. "Come over here and let me show you how it's done."

HOURS LATER, with my head swirling from all the information he's dumped on me, I head home. When I turned twenty, I told them I wanted to move out on my own, much to my aunt's dismay. They both finally agreed with the caveat being that I live nearby. I smile remembering how many houses we looked at before finding a three-bedroom cottage near the lake. It's close enough to the cabins that I keep ready for our monthly visitors, but private enough that I get my solitude. "I'm so tired," I mumble to myself as I pull into my driveway. "I sure hope Uncle Jesse knows what he's doing letting me handle everything."

My mind drifts back to when I was a kid. Uncle Jesse is my mom's brother and when he stopped by one day and saw me trying to find something to eat while my mom was passed out on the couch, he went ballistic. He and Aunt Carla couldn't have kids and he gave my mom an ultimatum - either shape up or let me stay with them. I feel my heart clench when I recall how she waved at me before telling him they could have me. I was six years old, underweight, somewhat sickly, and scared of my own shadow.

Uncle Jesse helped me pack my few belongings, grabbed what he called important paperwork, then took me home to Aunt Carla. Despite the nightmares and odd behaviors I had, neither of them gave up on me. I feel the tears falling as I recall the nights that Aunt Carla laid beside me on my bed, rubbing my back as I cried from the nightmares. I didn't stop hoarding food under my bed until Uncle Jesse started taking me grocery shopping with him. Once I realized that there would always be food, my incessant need to hide extra food stopped. It took a lot of love, therapy, and patience for me to believe that I was loved, had value, and was worthy. But neither of them ever gave up on me, pouring their energies into making sure that the emotional damage my mother did was dealt with so I could grow up happy and whole.

"And here I am today," I say as I pull into my garage. I still have my insecurities and self-doubts, but overall, I'm okay. I pull into the garage, park my car and close the overhead door, reflecting once again how I love the way the builders added a garage onto the cottage in such a way that you can't tell what it is from the outside once I close the door. When I go inside, there's a small mudroom that leads into my laundry room. My kitchen runs off the end of the hallway and leads into the great room. The master bedroom is down one hallway and pretty much goes the width of the house. The other two bedrooms, as well as a second bathroom are down the other hallway. I've made it into a cozy, warm environment; one I love coming home to. "Where's my Gizmo?" I call out as I set my purse and keys on the kitchen island. I hear a soft meow before I feel something bumping against my leg. Crouching, I reach out and pet my cat. "Hey, little man, are you hungry?" I ask. Another meow has me grinning as I pick him up and carry him over to his bowl. I leave dry food down all day, but he gets wet food in the morning and when I get home. "So, what'll be tonight? Salmon? Ocean whitefish? Chicken?" I muse, looking in the cupboard that's full of cans of his wet food. With each comment, he meows louder until I finally say, "Fine, chicken it is."

Now that the cat's happy, I can get changed into comfortable clothes before I cook dinner. It's not always easy to cook for one person, but Aunt Carla taught me that I could freeze a lot of dishes for later, and also pack leftovers for lunch. With my food issues from my childhood, I still worry about having enough, even though I no longer hide food under my bed. "Wonder what's on tonight?" I muse as I heat up some leftover chicken and dumplings. Grabbing some water, I carry my bowl back into my room and prepare to veg out.

When the alarm on my phone goes off, I grab it and notice that it's time to make sure the three cabins I take care of are clean. I generally go over after our visitors have left and do the laundry; this is to make sure that the cabins are aired out and to restock perishable items in the fridge. Looks like tomorrow will be a busier day than I anticipated. I pull my tablet over and place an online order so I can pick it up during my lunch hour. Best thing in the world that stores did was start online shopping with pickup because I hate shopping.

With that task done, I set my alarm for the next morning and turn out the light, leaving the TV on. I still have to have noise at night in order to sleep.

Dax

THE PULL of the moon wakes me from my slumber. I find myself sleeping more and more between my land time and I worry that at some point, I won't wake up at all. However, I'm an eternal optimist and hold out hope that my mate is out there. "I just haven't found her yet," I mutter. "Maybe this month."

CHAPTER 2
DAX

Two Days Later

The hardest part about the curse, for me, is trying to cram as much as possible into two or three days. As I make my way to the shore, I see my brethren doing the same. Each of us is on a mission, one that we make every single month. "Do you ever get tired of this?" I hear.

Turning, I see my cousin, Dayven. "Yeah, sometimes. But what other choice do we have?" I ask. "If we don't come out, we'll never find our mate. If we do come out but don't return, we'll die."

"Well, maybe this month is the one," he replies. "See ya in a few." With a wave of his hand, he heads off to his cabin to get dressed and likely, to head into town. I nod as I reach shore and start walking to my cabin. When I reach it, I find the hidden key and unlock the door.

"Home sweet home," I mutter. The irony is that even though I'm gone more than I'm here, the cabin is always fresh smelling when I arrive each month. Must be the caretaker. Whoever it is does a damn good job of replacing things that are needed, that's for sure. I head into the kitchen to grab a beer before I hit the shower. I know I just spent the last month sleeping, but the fact is that the change from merman to human is exhausting and I need to sleep for a little bit before I do anything else.

AWAKE NOW AND FULLY RESTED, I head into

town to grab something to eat. While my cabin is stocked, I have to go by the tattoo shop and meet with Jesse about the back piece I want. "Morning, Sheriff," I say as I pass by the town's sheriff. He's a bit older, with salt and pepper hair, but he knows what goes on in Aurora Falls and keeps a watch over our cabins when we're gone.

"Morning, Dax. Must be that time of the month, huh?" he asks.

"Yes, sir. I'm sure you've figured that out already."

He chuckles and nods. "Not too difficult when I see an influx of folks I haven't seen in a month. Take it easy, you hear?"

"Absolutely. Gonna grab something to eat then hit Mountain Ink and meet with Jesse." He starts to say something then shakes his head.

"Enjoy your time, Dax. If I don't see you before you go back, I'm sure I'll see you next month."

I nod and continue on my way. Being under water more than I'm above-ground has my calendar a bit off and I'm startled to see that Main Street is decorated for

Halloween. I had noticed a slight chill in the air, I guess it didn't dawn on me that it was fall already. I make a mental note to pull out my heavier clothes for the following month, because November is generally brutal temperature-wise.

Once at the diner, I place my order and look around. One of the nice things about Aurora Falls is that nothing ever really changes. There've been a few new businesses over the years, but for the most part, they're the same ones that have been around since the town was established.

"How's it going, Dax?" Eric, the local vet, asks. I nod at his wife, Ailani. She used to be one of us until she found Eric. Or rather, until he found her since he was the one that saw the mate mark we all bear.

"Just getting my bearings, Eric," I reply, sipping my coffee. "How have you two been?"

"Good. Been busy at the clinic, of course, but other than that, I can't complain."

"Always good to be busy, though," I state.

He nods, saying, "That's true. Well, I won't keep you,

I'm sure you've got stuff to do." He gives me a wink as if to say he knows my time is limited. I smirk, because his woman practically fell at his feet.

The waitress arrives with my food and I practically inhale it. When I'm underwater, I'm not hungry; it has something to do with the curse, I believe. But every month, I feel as if I can't get enough to eat. Once done, I toss down some money and head out to Mountain Ink.

Racine

UNCLE JESSE and Aunt Carla left last night, so I decide to get an early start at the shop this morning. Happy with the state of our inventory, I start turning on lights to let people know we're open, then head into the break room to grab something to drink. I need my morning caffeine, something that Uncle Jesse teases me about, but I can't stand coffee. Love the smell, but nothing I've ever added has made it even remotely palatable to me. "Ah, he stocked up for me," I murmur as I pull open the fridge and see the bottles of my favorite diet soda. Grabbing one, I'm about to go check the books to see who I have coming in when I hear the bell over the door ring, signifying that someone has walked in.

"I'll be right there," I call out as I hurry toward the front of the shop. When I see the man standing there, my heart starts hammering in my chest. He's tall without being overbearing, and his body type is what I've always looked for in a man. Not too muscular; maybe the word beefy would be more appropriate. He looks like he has the strength to pick me up and carry me, but he also looks soft enough to cuddle up against.

Where in the hell are these thoughts coming from?

Shaking my head, I approach him. "Hi, can I help you?" I ask. He turns his beautiful chocolate-brown eyes toward me and smiles.

"I'm looking for Jesse," he replies. Damn, he's one of Uncle Jesse's customers. I'd love to get my hands on his skin, but know if he's had my uncle, he won't want to switch over to me.

"Uh, well, he had to go out of town on personal business. I'm his niece, Racine. Can I help you with something?"

"He and I were meeting to talk about a back piece I want him to do for me."

My eyes widen when I remember the image that Uncle Jesse showed me. "Oh! You're Dax, right?" I question. At his nod, I continue, "He left a picture for you to look at. Let me go grab it." I rush into my uncle's office and find the folder he left on his desk. Grabbing it, I turn and head back to the lobby. "Here it is," I say, handing him the folder. "I'll understand if you want to wait for him to do the work, but I'll be honest and let you know that I don't know how long he'll be gone."

He raises a brow at me and asks, "Are you a tattoo artist as well?"

I nod before replying, "Yes. I've been laying ink since I was sixteen, actually. But if you've had Uncle Jesse in the past, you'll probably want to wait for him."

"No, this is my first one, so if you're up for it, you can do it," he says, looking over the transfer that Uncle Jesse drew. "I really like what he created." I glance at the tattoo and admire the image that my uncle has created. It's a giant, old-world looking map, with a compass that virtually pops out. Uncle Jesse has notes on the side regarding colors to use, and he also suggests watercoloring the area around the compass itself. "Can you do this?" he inquires.

"Yes, I can. Are you good with the colors he's suggesting?" I secretly hope he is because with his skin tone, the tattoo is going to be epic.

"I believe so, yes. When can you start?" I hold up a finger and go over to the desk to check my calendar.

"I have some time this morning and again this afternoon, if you'd like," I reply.

"Then let's do it before I chicken out." I giggle at the thought of this big, strapping man being afraid of anything. He almost looks like those Vikings on that television show and I can't wait to get my hands on his skin.

Down, girl. I have no idea why the presence of this particular man is causing such internal havoc; I've never had this reaction to a man before. "Follow me, Dax," I say, walking toward my station. I adjust my table so he can lie down flat and take the picture my uncle drew. "I'll be right back; I'm going to put this on a transfer. Go ahead and remove your shirt and get comfortable."

When I get back with the transfer, he's lying on the chair and I take in a deep breath at the thoughts that are swirling in my head. I've never had this kind of reaction to anyone, so I'm not sure how to handle it, except to stay professional. "Where were you thinking of having this?" I ask as I approach the chair.

"I'd like it on the right side," he replies. "That way, if I ever add anything to it, it can go on the left."

"Okay. I need to prepare your back first," I advise, pulling on gloves.

"What does that entail?" he asks.

"I need to wipe down the area and shave where the tattoo will be located. I promise, I won't cut you," I tease, the joke out before I can stop myself. I'm so used to the normal clientele that it doesn't dawn on me that he might think I was serious.

His laughter ringing out makes me sigh in relief. "I trust you won't cut me," he finally says. I nod even though he can't see me and begin working. Normally, I carry on a conversation when I'm tattooing someone, but this time, I have no clue what to talk about, so I stay silent.

Finally, after I've shaved him and placed the transfer, I say, "I've got the transfer placed. Go ahead and check it out and let me know if it's where you want it." He stands and stretches, and again, I want to cuddle close to him. Shaking my head, I wait to hear what he has to say.

He walks over to the three-way mirror I have set up in the corner of my station and turns around. I watch as he moves, captivated by his rugged good looks.

Get a grip, Raci. You're a fucking professional!

"I like it. You're starting now, right?" he asks.

I nod, turning to gather the inks I'll need. "I can get the outline done now, then we can add the colors later."

"I'm good, Racine." The sound of my name on his lips makes me sigh. Dammit, this may be the most challenging tattoo I've ever done!

Once I have everything together and a new pair of gloves on, I start the gun. "Are you ready?" I question.

"Yeah," he replies, his eyes closed. I glance over and

notice he's got the longest eyelashes I've ever seen and nearly swoon.

"Alright, let me know if it gets to be too much or if you need a break. I want to try and get all the outlining done this morning. Then, you can take a break and grab something to eat while I take care of two other customers."

"Let's do this."

I'm soon lost in the familiar drone of my gun as I move back between the ink and his back. "You doing okay?" I murmur, my concentration on the compass which needs to appear to pop out of his skin.

"So far, so good."

I smile and continue, the minutes evolving into half an hour, then an hour. Finally, at the two-hour mark, I shut my gun off and sit back, stretching to ease the kinks out of my neck and shoulders. "Let me wipe this first part down and you can take a look while I clean up for my next client," I advise. Once I have him wiped down, I start the process of sterilizing my work-station and getting ready for my next client while he stands and goes over to the mirror again. "Do you like it so far?" I ask, anxious to hear his thoughts. I put my own spin on things, making the edges of the map look a bit more ragged than the picture that Uncle Jesse drew. I feel like I'm holding my breath as he turns and stares at his back.

Long minutes pass and I feel sweat start pooling between my breasts. He finally turns and looks at me and says, "I like the changes you made a lot. Do you need to cover it or anything?"

I nod. "If you'll come over here, I'll put a light wrap on it to keep it from drying out. Give me about three hours and come back and I'll add the color."

He smiles and once again, I'm struck by how handsome he is. "I'll be back. Do you want me to bring you anything?"

"No, I generally pack a lunch. I'll heat it up between clients."

"Then I'll see you in a few hours." He waves as he walks out and I finally take a deep breath. Jesus, he's potent as hell and I hope like anything that he lives in the area because I want to get to know him better. I'm not sure how to accomplish that because I'm beyond shy, but maybe one of my friends will have some ideas.

THREE HOURS LATER, I'm in the breakroom heating up my lunch. I figure I have maybe ten or fifteen minutes to eat, hit the bathroom, then grab something to drink before Dax returns. While my food heats, I dash into the bathroom and relieve my aching bladder. I think this is another industry where we push ourselves to the edge and our bodies suffer. Making a mental resolve to do better, I wash my hands then head back into the break room to eat. With the fork poised at my mouth, I hear the bell over the door ring and groan. Guess I'll wait a bit longer to eat. Walking to the front, I smooth my shirt down and smile when I see Dax standing there.

"Hey, you're just in time," I state, motioning for him to follow me back to my station.

He sniffs the air and replies, "Did I catch you eating?"

"It's okay. I told you three hours. It's not your fault that the first client ran a bit late."

"Racine, go ahead and eat," he says. "I don't mind one bit."

I bite my lower lip while looking up at him. "Are you

sure? It's not very professional of me to keep you waiting."

"Do you have anyone after me?" I shake my head in response to his question and he says, "Then there's no issue as far as I'm concerned. I have nothing else planned, so waiting a few minutes until you finish eating is no skin off my back."

I smile. "Thank you, Dax."

"Not a problem. Now, go eat."

Grinning, I head back to the breakroom and my yummy spaghetti. "Make yourself comfortable. I'll be done in a few."

Dax

I GRIN as I hear the moans coming from the break-room. I knew she was hungry because I heard her stomach growling when she approached me. I may be an asshole at times and bossy to boot, but there's no way I'll let any woman go hungry just to take care of something I need. Well, unless we were occupied in bed, that is. Then I'd slake one hunger before taking care of any physical one she had.

I shake my head at that wayward thought. While I find my curvy tattoo artist attractive as hell, I'm not going to go there. Besides, if she were my intended mate, wouldn't she have seen my mark on my left inner bicep? Shrugging, I remove my shirt and get comfortable on the chair once again. I'm glad that I'm face down because her touch on my back causes a reaction I don't think she needs to see.

"Oh good, you're all ready," she says, coming into the room and interrupting my thoughts. "Let me just get the colors together and we'll start again."

"That works." Deciding to make some small talk, I ask, "You lived here all your life?"

"Yeah, well, since I was about six or so. My uncle came and got me and moved me in with him and my aunt. Grew up going to school here and hearing all the local legends, of course," she replies. I can hear the slight noises she makes as she readies the inks she'll need to put around the compass.

"Local legends?" I haven't told her I'm from here and

I'm curious to hear what's being said about our quaint but unique little town.

"You've never heard of the witch's curse?" she asks. "Well, about a thousand years ago, there was a witch who ruled this area who, in a fit of anger over how she was treated, cursed a boatload of Vikings to live at the bottom of the lake as mermaids and mermen. Legend says that if they meet their mate, they'll return to living on the land once again." She grins at me and I see the sparkle in her eyes.

"Do you believe these legends?"

"Well, I'm the caretaker for several of the cottages for our monthly visitors and I see the evidence that they've been there when I go by, so yeah, I guess I do believe."

"Sounds...interesting," I state, grinning. "What does that entail? The caretaking, I mean."

"I have three cottages I take care of each month. Right before the full moon, I make sure that the occupants have fresh food and any drinks they prefer. Once they've gone back, I go back and clear out anything that will spoil, wash their linens and clothes and get the houses ready for the next month."

I wonder if she's the one who takes care of my cabin, but I'm not about to out myself. I catch a whiff of the scent she wears and realize that she *is* the one who makes sure my favorite beer is stocked and my sheets are soft, not scratchy. I wonder if she's my mate? I won't ask, of course, because she has to be the one who sees the mark. I haven't left it covered, but her focus has been on the tattoo, so it's possible that she hasn't seen it yet.

"Sounds like you keep busy then," I remark.

"Between the clients that come in during tourist season and keeping up with the cottages, I do."

"What do you do for fun?"

"I'm mostly a homebody. I have a cat named Gizmo and once I'm done working, I usually hang at home and watch movies. Kind of boring to most, I'm sure."

I glance at her and see her face drawn in concentration as she prepares my back once again before she starts. "Do you enjoy your life?" I question.

"Mostly, yes. I mean, I get lonely sometimes because most of my friends are either married or they're seeing someone, and I don't want to be a third wheel. But outside of that, I do enjoy my life. I guess I'm just a homebody."

"I don't see anything wrong with that," I reply, trying not to flinch at the coldness of whatever it is she's using to clean my back.

"Sorry it's cold," she says. "If we hadn't had to take a break in the middle, you wouldn't have to suffer through it a second time."

I laugh because despite it being my first tattoo, I really didn't feel that much while she was working on me. There were a few spots that were a bit more tender than others, but overall, I've lived through worse. "If that's the worst of it this afternoon, we're good."

She giggles and I become entranced at the musical sound. I won't, however, start anything with her because once I do find my mate, I'll stay in Aurora Falls and that would be awkward. "You ready?" she asks.

"As I'll ever be," I respond.

I'm soon lost once again in the hum of her tattoo gun as she methodically shades different areas, while putting splotches of color on others. Before I know it, two hours have passed. I hear the gun shut off then she says, "All finished. Let me clean it up and you can look at it before I wrap it up."

"Sounds good." She quickly and efficiently wipes my back down then removes her gloves, motioning to me that I can get up. I stand and stretch and don't miss her sideways glance. Walking over to the three-way mirror, I turn so I can see my back and I am blown away. The sketch that Jesse drew was stunning, but what Racine has done has made it come to life. "Fuck, this is phenomenal," I state, turning toward her.

"Thank you. I'm glad you like it," she replies as she continues to clean her station. "Here, let me get you wrapped up." I stand motionless as she puts on another pair of gloves before smearing something on the tattoo then taping a gauze pad over it. She hands me some aftercare instructions and a tube of lotion and says, "Let me get you checked out. Once it heals up, if you want, come by and I'll touch up any areas if they need it free of charge."

I walk up to the front and she gets me checked out. "Thanks again, Racine. I love the look of it," I say.

"You're welcome. If you have any questions or prob-lems, let me know."

"I will. Good night."

"Night, Dax."

I walk away from one of the most captivating women I've ever met cursing the fact that I'm unable to pursue anything.

CHAPTER 3
RACINE

After Dax leaves, I finish cleaning then close the shop for the night. Before I go, I look over the book to see what I can expect the next day. I've found that with the chaos of my early childhood, I prefer being organized and prepared. Something I'm sure no one will ever want to deal with, along with my million other quirks.

Whatever, Racine, you're probably destined to be alone except for a house full of cats.

I call an order in to the diner, too tired to cook, then stop in and pick it up before heading home. Once home, I hear the plaintive meows of Gizmo and grin. "Who's a hungry boy?" I ask, making my way into the kitchen. He rubs against my legs and I crouch down to give him a good rubdown before standing and opening the cabinet to grab a can of food. "Looks like ocean whitefish tonight," I remark, opening the can and dumping it into the waiting bowl. He meows then shoves his face in the bowl. "Well, alrighty then," I mumble. Grabbing my bag from the diner, I head into the bedroom to get changed.

Looks like another thrilling night. Me, Netflix, and my cat.

MY RINGING PHONE wakes me up just before my alarm is due to go off the next morning. "Hello?" I know my voice is groggy sounding, but when someone wakes you up at seven in the morning, they deserve whatever they get, right?

"Hey, sweetheart. Was trying to call before you got your day started," Uncle Jesse says.

"Perfect timing then, because my alarm hasn't gone off yet."

He chuckles then asks, "How was your first solo day?"

"Not too bad. Some guy named Dax came in and he was okay with me inking your design. I made a few small changes to it, but he really liked how it looked."

"Good, good. Did you take a picture?"

I nod then remember he can't see me. "Yeah. Hang on a sec and I'll send it to you." I quickly send him the pictures I took of Dax's tattoo then put the phone on speaker so I can get my bed made. Another of my quirks; I have to make my bed when I first get up. Probably comes from only having a mattress on the floor and one blanket, who knows? Although, once I went to live with my aunt and uncle, I chose to make my bed because the one they got me was so special, I felt I needed to do it. I grab the trash from my meal the night before and head into the kitchen to make a cup of tea. I try to limit my caffeine intake to when I'm at the shop, although on the weekends, all bets are off as a rule.

"That looks fucking phenomenal, Raci!" Uncle Jesse states.

"You think so?" I hate sounding insecure when it comes to my tattooing, but sometimes I am and the piece I did on Dax is the biggest one I've done on my own to date.

"Hell yeah. I wasn't worried about leaving the shop in your care while we're gone but now I am because when some of my customers see this, they're going to want you to do their ink."

I start giggling. "No they won't, Uncle Jesse! They're loyal to you."

"You ready for the festival this weekend?"

"Yeah, I have to go in a bit early to put up the supplies that were delivered yesterday. I bet we have a lot of flash art."

"Probably so based on last year's business," he replies. From October through February, Aurora Falls has festivals that bring the tourists in in droves. This month, with it being Halloween, folks will be in and shopping for fall decorations and trying to find unique items for gifts for Christmas.

"Then I better get busy. Love you guys," I say.

"We love you too. Call me if you need me, you hear?" he instructs.

"Yes, sir," I reply, grinning.

TODAY HAS BEEN HOPPING and once again, I leave the shop exhausted but also exhilarated. Since it's Saturday and the shop is closed tomorrow, I decide to eat at the diner and am soon seated at a booth. When the bell rings over the door, I look up and see Dax walking in and immediately, my pulse quickens. He walks over and asks, "Can I sit with you?" I glance around and see that most of the tables and booths are occupied.

"Sure, there's plenty of room," I reply. He grins at me and sits down before grabbing a menu.

I've ordered my drink but not my food, so when the waitress returns, she takes both of our orders, as well as his drink order and promises she'll get it out as quickly as possible. "Were you busy today?" he asks.

"It was steady. The festival generally draws in the tourists who mostly want flash art."

"Flash art?" he questions.

"Yeah, you know, hearts, butterflies, skulls. Easy things."

"Ah, gotcha."

"How's yours doing?" I inquire, sipping my water. I try not to drink sodas after a certain time each day and switch to water at night. It's my attempt at being healthy.

"It's good. I had a little bit of a challenge getting the lotion on this morning, but found my cousin and forced him into helping me."

I giggle, saying, "Bet he was thrilled to do that for you."

"He gave me some shit, but when he saw it, he said he might just have to get one done now."

"Like yours?"

"Yeah, except just the black and maybe gray."

"That would look pretty cool too, I think," I say.

"If you say so," he replies. "Oh, good, food's here. I'm starved." I nod at his words because I am as well.

"Thanks, Susie," I tell the waitress once she puts the plates down.

"No problem, Raci. You guys need anything else?" she asks.

"I'm good. How about you, Dax?" I question.

"Just keep the water coming and I'll be happy," he replies, winking at our waitress. I feel something strange happen when he does that and don't understand the sensation. It almost feels like jealousy, only I have nothing to compare it to since I've never been jealous of anyone in my life. Even as a small child, I didn't get upset if someone had something I wanted. For starters, I wasn't out and about much when I lived with my mother. Then, when I moved in with Uncle Jesse and Aunt Carla, they made sure I had everything I needed and a lot of what I wanted.

"You got it," she tells him, a flush creeping up her face. I wonder if she's more his type; she's taller than me and even though I'm quite sure her boobs are fake, they're big and I'm pretty sure most men like that kind of thing.

As we eat, he asks me more questions about the town,

but offers very little information about himself, causing me to suspect that maybe he's just visiting. He did mention a cousin, after all. Once our meal is done, he motions for Susie and asks for the check. "Oh, you don't have to get mine," I say.

"I absolutely do," he replies. "There wasn't a spot to sit when I got here, and you let me crash your booth."

I roll my eyes. "That sounds kind of lame to me."

"Regardless, I'm taking care of the bill and I'll walk you to your car since it's dark out."

"Oh, and I thought chivalry was dead," I tease, grinning.

"Never when there's a pretty woman around."

Dax

AFTER I WALK Racine to her car, I head back to my cabin, my thoughts steeped in her. I don't know what there is that draws me to her but I need to stop because she's a sweet girl and I'll only break her heart. "Dax, hey, Dax!" my cousin calls out.

Turning, I scowl at him. He's apparently partying this month and is stumbling toward me, a bottle of rum dangling between his fingers. "What in the hell are you doing, Dayven?" I ask, motioning to the bottle.

"Enjoying my visit topside," he slurs, taking a gulp.

"Seems to me you've had enough, man," I tell him, grabbing for the bottle. Once I have it, I reach for him. "Let me walk you home. You'll thank me tomorrow for not getting into trouble with the sheriff."

"Fine, whatever," he grouses. "Spoilsport."

"We've got maybe one more day, Dayven," I remind him. "You don't need to be locked up when it's time to go back. Unless you're ready to call it quits?" I ask.

"Fuck that noise! No, I'm not giving up. I just want to have fun this month. I doubt my mate is here for the festival or anything like that."

THE PULL TO go back is sooner than I expect.

Before I leave, I write a note for my caretaker thanking them for taking such good care of my home while I'm away. Unfortunately, I have to head back to the lake without seeing Racine again. Oh well, I've got her image committed to memory. If nothing else, it'll keep me occupied over the next month.

CHAPTER 4
ONE MONTH LATER

Dax

Arriving at the cabin, I walk in and smile. Home, sweet home, at least for the next three days. Walking into the kitchen, I see that my note from last month is gone and there's one in its place. I grab a beer before picking it up and lean against the counter to read.

. . .

DEAR DAX,

I appreciate the note. Honestly, it's no problem at all; it's what I'm called to do. Please let me know if there's anything that you'd like in particular and I'll make sure to stock it for you for next month's visit. I hope you find your mate soon.

Racine

FINDING out that Racine is my caretaker settles something deep inside and I wonder how she feels knowing that she's been taking care of me all this time? Then I wonder why I'm concerned with how she feels. Jesus, I'm so screwed. Taking my beer with me, I grab a quick shower then flop onto my bed. Once I wake from my nap, I'll go to the tattoo shop so she can look at my tattoo and also so I can talk to her in person. Maybe she'll have time to fix one area that I scraped against a rock.

Racine

MY EYES LOOK at the calendar and I realize that it's once again the full moon. I wonder if Dax has made it to his cabin and found my note. I was shocked as hell when I went last month and found his note to me, even though he didn't know it was me in particular who takes care of his cabin. Without conscious thought, I pull it from my pocket and read it once again. It's well-worn because I've looked at it more times than I care to admit.

DEAR CARETAKER,

I don't know who you are, but I wanted to thank you for taking such good care of me. When I arrive every month, I know that my favorite beer will be in the refrigerator, my bed will be freshly made, and anything I've used will be replaced. I don't know if you take care of anyone else's cabin or not, but if you do, I'm sure they feel the same way. Take care.

Sincerely,

Dax

"RACI? GIRL, ARE YOU DAYDREAMING

AGAIN?" Uncle Jesse asks, coming up to the front counter where I'm supposed to be checking the book to see who we've got coming in today.

"What? Um, no, not really," I reply.

"Bullshit," he grins. "I'm hoping that Dax comes in this month so I can see that tat in living color."

I shiver because I hope he does as well. Even knowing he likely belongs to someone else, there's just some-thing about him that calls to me. "Who knows?" I blithely reply. "If he does, I'm sure he'll be happy to show you." I want to see it as well and make sure nothing needs to be touched up.

"He won't have a choice," Uncle Jesse says. "I think that's one of the best tats to come out of this shop since I opened it. I knew you had it in your blood, Raci. You've always done good work, but his tattoo has taken your abilities to another level as far as I'm concerned."

"Thanks, Uncle Jesse. Um, we have a pretty steady book today. Do you want me to place an order at the diner for lunch? I can run out and pick it up between clients."

"What's today, Wednesday?"

"Yes, sir."

"Then it's meatloaf day," he replies. "Go ahead and do that; we can always reheat it if we catch a walk-in client."

"I'm on it," I tell him. "Uncle Jesse?"

"What, Raci?"

"Did I tell you that Dax is one of the lake visitors?"

He grins and shakes his head. "No, but you told your Aunt Carla, so I know. I also know that you've been the one taking care of his cabin, and that you find him intriguing and attractive."

"Yeah, but nothing can come of it, Uncle Jesse. I mean, if I was his mate, wouldn't I have seen his mark last month?"

"Not necessarily, sweetheart. Just depends on where it's located." He grins at me when my face turns red imagining just where his mark could be.

"Well, I'm not going to ask to inspect his body," I mumble. I don't think I'd have the guts, that's for sure! But he sure has starred in my nightly dreams. So much so that I wake most mornings all sweaty and filled with desire.

Uncle Jesse bursts into laughter at my words before wagging his finger at me. "Girl, I better keep my eye on you! You're getting sassy!"

Deciding that a subject change is in order, I ask, "Do you want me to create a few new flash art pieces to put in the book? I know the Christmas festival isn't until next month, but I thought maybe I'd start working on the advertising and wanted to create a few holiday-themed tats for those folks who are really into it. What do you think?"

He doesn't say anything for so long that I worry I over-stepped somehow. Finally, he says, "I think that's a great idea, honey. Let me see them when you're done, and we'll get it all loaded up on the social media sites. What do you think of us offering a special price for flash art tattoos next week for Black Friday?"

"I like it; what were you thinking cost-wise?"

"Let's say thirty dollars for flash art, which is a twenty-dollar savings. You up for being that busy?"

"Yeah. I want to be able to donate money to Eric for the animal clinic so he can defray adoption costs."

"How about this? I'll donate what I make on any flash art pieces I do as well."

"I think he's going to love us since he mostly covers the costs himself. Maybe I can work that into the ad? You know, put something like 'All proceeds from flash art tattoos will be donated to Triton's Veterinary Clinic'. What do you think?"

"Write it up, Raci-girl. We might make that a permanent thing since I had no clue he did that out of his own pocket."

"I found out when I had Gizmo there for his shots and Ailani brought in a stray she saw down at the lake."

"Get busy, honey," he instructs.

"I'm on it, Uncle Jesse." I shake my head at his antics; for whatever reason, he and Aunt Carla have both been more relaxed since returning from dealing with Grandpa Paul's estate. I know he said they have something for me, but we've all been so busy, I told them to just wait and tell me on Thanksgiving.

Our morning flies by and before I know it, I'm walking

down to the diner to pick up our lunch. While waiting at the counter for them to bag it up, I hear, "Racine?" and turn, seeing Dax standing there.

"Hi, Dax. How've you been?" I ask, ignoring the fact that my pulse is now racing.

"Good. You?"

"Same. Busy, of course. Just came by to pick up our lunch," I reply.

"Do you have any time today? I need you to touch up a spot that I scraped against a rock."

I grin because I'm sure he did it when he returned to the lake. Nodding, I say, "It's pretty steady today, but I'll work you in. Besides, Uncle Jesse wants to see the tattoo for himself. He said the pictures probably don't do it justice."

"They don't," he replies. Leaning in, he says, "I saw that you got my note."

My face heats up and I know I'm blushing. "I did, yes. I had no idea you were who I was taking care of these past few years. I took over for my aunt since her at-home business picked up. I helped her growing up, so it made sense to do that instead of finding someone else since I was already familiar with the process."

"Well, I'll repeat what I said. I do appreciate everything you do each month, especially since I've only got forty-eight to seventy-two hours max, you know?"

I nod, even though I can't fathom having such a short time period available to meet my fated mate. "I take it since you're back this month that you had no luck last month," I state.

"No." He looks a bit disgruntled when he tells me this and I find myself patting his arm in commiseration.

"Well, maybe you will this month," I say, trying to be as positive sounding as possible. I don't know who she is but I kind of already hate her for taking the first-ever man I've felt the slightest attraction to away from me. Stupid, huh?

"Maybe, who knows?"

The waitress running the counter comes over with my bag and says, "That'll be fifteen dollars, Racine. Do you want to pay it or put it on your uncle's tab?"

I grin because Uncle Jesse is one of the few who runs a monthly tab at the diner for our meals when we're working, but he always has me leave a tip right then. "Put it on the tab, Shelly, please," I reply, handing her a ten. "This is for you."

"You know you guys don't have to do that," she states.

"Yes, we do. You guys take great care of us. Hell, last week, you had Davy deliver it to us when we couldn't get out, remember? It's the least we can do."

"Well, we appreciate it," she replies, finally pocketing the money.

I turn toward Dax and say, "I'll see you later at the shop, Dax."

"Absolutely. Now go eat; you look thinner than last month." My eyebrows raise because I have lost weight. I wasn't trying to do so; we've just been really busy, so eating has been sporadic some days. Plus, I started taking a kickboxing class and some of my more jiggly spots are firming up. He sees my expression and quickly says, "Not that you needed to lose weight because you didn't. I just noticed that your shirt appears to be loose."

"Well, I'm not sure how to take it, but I'm not

offended. It's been a bit hectic this past month, and I started working out," I reply.

He leans in and says, "You're perfect just the way you are and any man who says otherwise is a fool."

I shake my head at him and state, "I'll be sure to let the hordes knocking down my door know that fact. See you later." With that, I walk out of the diner and head back to the shop, eager to tuck into the homemade meatloaf that puts Aunt Carla's to shame.

Dax

I GRIN at her retreating back before finally taking a seat at the counter. "Do you know what you'd like?" the waitress asks me.

"Can I have today's special?" I respond. "And a Coke."

"Sure, I'll go put your order in and then grab your drink."

"Thanks."

I watch the other customers as they come and go, lost in my thoughts. After all these years, I've pretty much resolved any lingering issues from my childhood, and of course, my adulthood has been spent underwater. "Hey, Dax," a voice calls out. Turning, I see my cousin, looking a helluva lot better than he did the last time I saw him.

"Hey yourself, Dayven. What're you up to?"

"Thinking about checking out that tattoo shop. Which one was it? I saw we have two here in Aurora Falls now."

"Mountain Ink," I reply, taking a sip of my drink. "Are you goofing off this month or are you getting serious?"

"Hell, I don't know. It feels almost foolish to keep look-ing, but I'm an eternal optimist, so I guess I'll look. In case I decide otherwise, will you check on me before you go back? I'd hate to miss out on a mate because I was hungover, you know?"

I start laughing at his almost fatalistic statement. "Yeah, I'll make sure you're with me. I won't leave you to your own devices."

"Good, good. So, what's good here?" he asks, sitting next to me.

"I'm getting the special today. It's meatloaf, mashed potatoes, green beans, and a roll."

"Sounds good." When the waitress returns with my plate, he asks, "Can I get one of those too? And lemonade to drink, if you have it."

"It's freshly squeezed," the waitress responds. "I'll be right back with your food."

We spend the next hour eating and killing time, just bullshitting about everything and nothing. "Have you noticed that they're getting ready for Thanksgiving?" Dayven remarks.

"That usually happens in November," I reply, smirking at him.

"Whatever. Just seems like stuff is moving faster and faster any more is all."

"Well, hold on to your hat because next month, it'll be December, so they'll have Christmas stuff up."

He grins and tosses his napkin at me. "C'mon, let's head out. I'm buying today," he says when I pull out my wallet. I nod but put down a few dollars for a tip because our waitress was good about keeping our drinks refilled.

After he pays, we walk down to the tattoo shop. I feel my pulse start jumping the closer we get, excited to see Racine again.

CHAPTER 5
DAX

We walk into the tattoo shop and my eyes immediately scan the area, looking for Racine. I have no idea why I've got such a strong attraction to her and I mentally vow to only look, not touch, since my primary focus needs to be on finding my mate whenever I'm topside, not chasing after her. "Hey, Dax!" Jesse calls out, coming into the reception area. "How've you been?" he asks, shaking my hand.

"Pretty good. This is my cousin, Dayven," I reply, waving my hand at my pain in the ass cousin. "He's thinking about getting the same tattoo, only in blacks and grays."

"I'm sure Raci can hook him up. Racine!" he yells.

"Be right there," she hollers. I grin because even speaking louder, her voice sends a thrill through me.

"She did a great job on mine," I admit.

"Yeah, I want to see it," Jesse states, motioning for me to raise my shirt. I pull my shirt over my head and turn, not missing the indrawn breath I hear behind me. Guess Racine isn't immune to me either. Good to know, even though it can't go anywhere. Dammit all to hell, Tamsin! Why'd you have to curse all of us? Of course, if she hadn't, I'd long be gone from this world and would never know this petite firecracker who is now standing behind me.

"I see I have some touch-up work to do," she murmurs. I feel her fingers lightly touch the tattoo and swallow a groan.

"Yeah, tangled with a rock," I admit. What I don't say is a bunch of us were assing around when we got back, swimming around and basically stirring up the bottom of the lake to the point I never saw the overhang.

"I've got some time now, if you do," she says. I turn and look down at her and notice that she's done something different with her hair.

"Your hair's different," I blurt out.

She smiles and says, "Yeah, Aunt Carla and I had an aunt-niece day out and went to a spa. Figured it was time to take off a few inches at least." She may have cut a few inches off, but it still falls to mid-waist in soft, tousled curls that have me clenching my hands to keep from reaching out. I bet it's soft and can imagine how it would feel entwined in my fingers as I pounded into her from behind.

"I like it." Dayven nudges me and when I look at him, he gives me a leer. Stupid ass. When she looks in his direction, I say, "This idiot here is my cousin, Dayven."

"Nice to meet you," she replies, holding out her hand.

"Can you do the same tattoo only in black and gray?" he asks instead of saying hello. I swear, when we were tossed into the lake by Tamsin, he must have hit his head or something because sometimes, he's a doofus.

"I can, yes. Did you want it done today?" she questions.

"Sure, why not," he says.

"I'm first," I state.

"Of course, let's get you to my station and I'll get it fixed for you," she replies. "Dayven, you can either wait or let Uncle Jesse take care of you."

"Doesn't matter to me. Whoever's got the time," he says.

"Then I'll get you taken care of while she fixes Dax's tat," Jesse states.

I nod as I follow her into her work area. Once I'm settled on her chair, I say, "Appreciate the decorations, Racine."

She blushes and then shocks me by saying, "I thought you might enjoy it. I hope I didn't overstep."

I roll to my side and take her hand in mine. "Not at all. Since you took over making sure my cabin is ready, I've noticed those little touches that make it look more homey. Coming in this month and seeing the small tree in the window was nice."

"I know it's a bit early for a Christmas tree, but I figured you don't get to enjoy it as long as the rest of us so that's why I put it up this month."

"Well, I appreciate it," I reply, releasing her hand and rolling back.

Racine

MY HEART RACES as I get things ready to fix his tattoo. I don't know what possessed me to decorate his cabin this year because I've never done it before, but there's something about him that calls to me. Once I have the inks ready, I don gloves and ask, "You ready?" At his nod, I pick up my tattoo gun and get started. As is usually the case, time passes quickly and soon, I'm wiping off the excess ink. "All fixed, Dax," I murmur, giving it a once-over. When I do, I see something shiny on his left bicep.

What the hell is that? I've never seen tattoo ink that practically shimmers! Leaning closer, I state, "I thought you said the compass and map was your first tattoo?"

"It is," he admits, his eyes closed.

"Then what's this?" I ask, reaching out to touch the tattoo I can visibly see. It almost looks like a Celtic knot, but the ink is shimmery. The second my fingers touch it, I start seeing what I can only describe as a running movie, one where I'm a spectator. I see Dax's memories of when the witch cursed them, the very air around her sparking with rage and grief. I see the serpent that is on the ship's bow turn into a living, breathing thing as it slips into the lake to serve as protector for the crew. I watch as the men and women collapse, writhing about on the deck as they transform into merpeople. As the movie in my head plays on, I see people I recognize from around the town and realize that they managed to break the curse. I see Dax, month after month, coming ashore only to return a few days later, shoulders slumped in defeat, and my heart cries out.

My pulse pounds as the movie reel goes faster and faster, showing some months where Dax doesn't bother coming to shore and others where he and his cousin spend their time drunk. "Racine?" His voice breaks through to me and I slowly blink at him, as the world spins on its axis.

I can't speak, my words are all jumbled in my brain. "Dax? I, we, um." I close my eyes and take a deep breath in and then blow it out before asking, "Does me seeing this mean what I think it does?"

"You can see my mark?" he questions.

"Yeah, it's right here," I reply, touching it again. Thankfully, my touch isn't accompanied by another head-rushing movie because seeing it once was heart-breaking enough.

"It does," he admits, looking at me. "And I'm glad it's you because since we first met last month, I've felt drawn to you, which concerned me since I didn't know you were my destined mate." He must see something on my face because he continues, "I wouldn't have ever pursued anything because that wouldn't have been fair to you or to whoever was my mate, of course. But knowing that it's you? Makes everything I've felt fall into place."

I don't know how to react right now. Finding out that this gorgeous man is mine is exhilarating and fright-ening at the same time. I've never dated all that much and am worried that I won't be enough for him. Only, how do I convey that to him so he understands? "I don't know what to say," I admit, my voice barely above a whisper.

"Can you take a break?" he asks, looking at me closely. "I think we should talk, and it looks like there's something on your mind."

I mentally think of the appointment book up front. I don't have any other clients scheduled and Uncle Jesse is more than capable of handling any walk-ins. "I can leave once I get you cleaned up and my station straightened for tomorrow. I need to let Uncle Jesse know too." He nods and I focus on getting his back cleaned up and wrapped. "There you go, Dax. If you give me about twenty minutes, I should be ready to go."

"That's fine, Racine. I'll go see how Dayven's getting on. Do you want me to talk to Jesse?"

"No, I'll take care of it." I feel like I'm in shock or something because his voice sounds like it's coming from a tunnel.

Dax stands and approaches me. "Racine? Are you okay? I know all of this is a huge shock to you. Please don't shut down on me."

"I don't mean to, Dax. It just seems so surreal is all. I never would have guessed that I would be someone's mate."

"Not someone's mate, *my* mate," he growls out, pulling me toward him. "I can't wait to do this any longer," he murmurs, as he lowers his face to mine.

Oh, my God! The second his lips touch mine, everything around us ceases to exist, except for the two of us. His tongue swipes across my lower lip and I gasp, allowing him entry. As the kiss heats up, I unconsciously move closer to him, seeking the warmth of his embrace. He keeps the kiss shorter than I would've liked, but there's so much promise hovering on the horizon that I shiver. I pull back slightly, breathless, and he grins down at me. "I think whatever I'm worried about won't be an issue," I whisper.

"You will never worry about anything again, Raci," he promises. "Now, get cleaned up in here and I'll meet you out in front, okay?"

I nod but don't verbally respond. Hot yet bossy.

Dax

AFTER CHECKING on Dayven's progress, I walk to the front of the shop and sit down to wait for Racine. I can't believe that after all these years, I've found my mate. I frown a bit when I recall her expression; something is bothering her and it's my job as her mate to find out what it is and fix it. "Are you ready?" she asks, breaking into my reverie.

I glance at her and smile. She still looks flustered from our kiss and I can't wait to see how hot and bothered I can get her when we're alone. "I am, yes," I reply. Standing, I take her hand and walk out to her car. "Where do you want to go?"

"My place? I need to check on Gizmo; he wasn't acting right this morning."

"Then let's go." Dayven and I walked into town, so I get in the passenger side of her car. She's petite, so it's a smaller one and I feel as though my knees are at my chest. Her giggles at my predicament have me looking over at her. "What's so funny? Doesn't everyone ride like this?"

"I think I'm going to need something bigger, huh?" she replies.

"Yes you will, because this isn't anything I can do long-term."

"I'll put it on my to-do list then," she quips. I like her sense of humor; she doesn't seem to be intimidated by my size, which is a good thing since we're mates.

The drive to her house doesn't take too long and soon we're pulling into her driveway. She parks the car in the garage and lowers the door before getting out. "I like the outside," I state as we walk into the house from the garage.

She glances up at me and smiles, saying, "Thank you. I've made it into a home. Well, I think so, at least." I hope she has because my cabin is utilitarian and if I have a choice, we'll live here. *Slow down, Dax, you just found one another.*

"Where's your cat?" I ask as we walk into the kitchen.

"I don't know. He's usually waiting for me in the kitchen. If you're thirsty, help yourself to whatever's in the fridge. I'll be right back. I need to find him."

I nod to show I understand and head over to the refrigerator. I know from getting the tattoo last month that I need to keep hydrated, so seeing bottled waters, I grab two and open the first one. While I wait, I glance around and notice all the touches that make this cottage a warm, inviting home. I see Racine walking back into the kitchen with a huge, rust-colored cat. "What kind of cat is it?" I inquire. I've never seen one with a smooshed-in face before.

"He's a Himalayan Persian," she replies, putting him down by the food dish. "C'mon, Gizzie, let Mama get you something to eat." I don't know much about cats but the meow he lets out sounds pitiful.

"Does he always sound like that?" I ask, my curiosity now roused.

"No." The look she gives me is equal parts worry and concern. "I think I need to call Eric."

"Who's that?" My ire raises at the mention of another man, and I can't help the small growl that slips out, causing her to raise her eyebrows at me.

"He's my vet, Dax. Nothing more, nothing less." I relax when she replies because I know that Eric is happily married to a fellow mermaid.

"Can he see him today?"

"I don't know. I'll call him if you're sure you don't mind?"

I shake my head. Now that I've found my mate, I'm content to just be with her. "Whatever you need to do, I'll go with you," I state.

She nods as she picks up her phone, presumably to call the vet. When her expression grows more concerned, I walk closer and pull her into my arms so her back is against my chest in an effort to bring her some comfort. I can't hear the vet's conversation, but after initially telling him what was going on with her cat, she's basically listened. "Okay, I'll be there shortly. Thanks, Eric," she finally says, disconnecting the call.

"I take it we're going to the vet?"

"We are, yes. That is, if you still don't mind coming with me?"

"Not at all, Racine."

CHAPTER 6
RACINE

D*on't cry. Whatever Eric says, don't cry and show Dax that you're weak.* I repeat this mantra to myself on the way to the vet. While it doesn't take long to get there, right now I feel like I've been on the road for hours. I'm so lost in my thoughts that it takes Dax grabbing my hand in his to break me loose. "I'm sorry, what?"

"I said that whatever was going on, I'll be with you," he repeats. "You're not alone any longer."

As if I can forget that this man is my mate! I glance at him quickly and reply, "I'm still not fully clear on all of that, either."

"When we get back from the vet's, we'll talk," he promises, giving my hand a squeeze. Truly, I'm not sure how we're able to hear one another because Gizmo is yowling from his carrier in the back seat.

I finally pull into the clinic and park, my hands shaking as I think about what could potentially be wrong with my baby. Uncle Jesse and Aunt Carla got him for me when he was six weeks old from a friend of theirs who was a breeder. He was the runt of the litter but has grown into a beautiful, loving pet. If anything is seriously wrong, I'm not sure how I'll handle it. I grab my keys, get out and then go to grab the carrier when Dax takes it from me. "I can carry it, Dax," I insist.

"I've got him, baby," he replies.

Baby. The sound of that directed toward me by him rolls over my senses and I barely resist the urge to shudder at the need that grips me. "Thank you."

He nods and takes my hand with his free one as we

walk to the door. Once inside, I see Eric at the counter. "Hey, Eric, got here as soon as I could."

"Racine, I called you less than ten minutes ago. Now, let's go into exam room two and let me take a look at Gizmo. Hey, Dax, good to see you again," he says, holding his hand out to Dax.

"Same. How's your family?" Dax replies, releasing my hand to take Eric's.

"They're doing well. Probably out rescuing more strays as we speak," Eric says as we get into the room.

"Knowing your wife like I do, you're probably right," Dax responds, causing Eric to raise his eyebrows at me.

I ignore Eric's look and get Gizmo out of his carrier. Ironically, he is now silent. "Okay, so he's not really eating and feeling him, he feels like he may have lost some weight," I confess. "I've noticed he's not finishing all of his wet food at night."

"Let's take a look," Eric says, his calm manner instantly setting me at ease. He gets him weighed then takes his vitals. After palpating his abdomen, he says, "I want to get a urine sample and also do a quick X-ray. I think I know what might be going on."

"What?" I can't help the panic in my tone and Dax must sense it because he moves close enough to me that I can feel the heat radiating from him.

"As male cats age, they're prone to developing kidney issues. He has a full bladder now, so I want to see if I'm right while gathering a sample to send off to culture."

I nod as I swallow back tears. "Okay. Is it going to hurt him?"

"No. It may tick him off, but that's just because he's a regal dude and they hate to suffer that type of indignity," he teases. I giggle because Gizmo *does* act like he's royalty most of the time, although at night, he turns into a cuddly teddy bear – one that purrs incessantly all night long. "Okay, I'll be back in a few minutes. Just sit tight," Eric says, picking Gizmo up. I love how gentle he is with the animals; he lightly ruffles Gizmo's fur and murmurs, "Let's get you fixed up, old man, so your mama will stop worrying."

I slump onto the bench that's in the room and Dax sits next to me, drawing me close to his side. He kisses my temple and whispers, "It'll be fine. If something's going on, you found out early enough, right?"

I nod. "Yeah, this is true." At least, I hope it's true. I

bring him in for his yearly check-up, of course, and buy the food that Eric recommends. I know that someday, he'll be gone, but I want to do my best to keep him as long as I can.

"I'VE NEVER HEARD of a cat developing chronic kidney disease," I tell Dax as we drive back to my house. I know there's a technical name for it, but Eric gave me the layman's term and that's what I'll use since I can't spell the disease much less pronounce it! "I'm glad Eric took the time to explain what it is and that he had the special food that Gizmo gets to eat from now on." I guess I'll go online to the place that I order food and snacks from and see if I can get the prescription food from them cheaper. If not, maybe Eric will give me a discount. He's good at making sure his clients can get what they need at affordable prices.

"Well, he gave you a lot of information," he replies, holding a sheaf of papers that Eric printed off for me to 'peruse at my leisure' as he put it.

"This is true," I say, pulling into my driveway. Once we're inside and I have Gizmo unloaded, I pick up the gravity feeder and toss the old food that's in it before replacing the dry food with the prescription brand that Eric sold me. "I still have a lot in this bag," I murmur. "I wonder if I can donate it to Eric to use for the strays he picks up."

"I'm sure it won't go to waste if you do that," Dax replies. "Now, let's eat so we can talk." I nod as I pull the takeout boxes from the bag he carried in. While I was waiting on the preliminary tests at the vet's office, Dax went down to the diner and picked up dinner for us.

"What would you like to drink?" I ask, opening the refrigerator.

"Beer if you have it," he replies. I grin and pull a bottle of beer out, as well as a bottle of water for myself. For some reason, I picked up a six-pack of the kind that Dax drinks when I went to the store.

We sit at the table in my breakfast nook but soon enough, we're done eating and everything is cleaned up. He grabs fresh drinks for both of us and takes my hand, leading me into the living room and over to the couch. Setting the drinks down, he sits then pulls me onto his lap so I'm straddling him. "Okay, let's talk about what had that look in your eyes earlier, Racine."

I look at him then look away. "I'm not really sure where to start, Dax," I confess.

"How about at the beginning? I'll let you get it all out then ask questions if I have any," he responds.

"Okay. Well, in the interest of full disclosure about what you'll be getting into with me, you should probably know it all." Taking a deep breath, I say, "When I was six years old, Uncle Jesse stopped by where I was living with my mother to check on me. What he found was so distressing that he told my mother that he and Aunt Carla were taking me so that I had a chance at a life."

Seeing his questioning look, I continue, "My mother wasn't a good one. We lived in the next town over in a place that can best be described as a hovel. I was underweight, sickly, and wasn't enrolled in school. My mother didn't want a child and claimed I ruined her life." Memories of that time flash through my head and I feel the tears well in my eyes when I remember how hard I tried as a little girl to get my mom's attention. "I also had some bruises that weren't from the normal playing that kids do, you know?"

I see anger flare in his eyes at my words and reach out

to touch his shoulder. "It's okay, Dax. It was a long time ago and Uncle Jesse and Aunt Carla were wonderful to me once we got through those first few months." The noise he makes has me grinning. "Anyhow, my mother didn't raise a fuss, just told him where the important papers were at and he helped me pack up my stuff." I really didn't have much in the way of clothes and the only toy I had was a baby doll that they had gotten me for my birthday.

"So, the next few months were hard; they were trying to get me healthy and Aunt Carla worked with me incessantly to teach me the basics I'd need for school. I had a room at their house already for the few times I was allowed to spend the night because my mother wanted to go out, but when I fully moved in, they let me decorate it. Uncle Jesse drew a mural on my wall, and I helped him paint it." I smile at that memory because Aunt Carla swore up and down that I wore more paint than the wall. I remember the laughter and teasing that slowly drew me out of my shell.

"They sound like wonderful people who love you very much," he remarks.

"They are and they do. I still had some health issues due to malnourishment and that led me to hoard food under my bed." He looks confused so I continue explaining, "My mother didn't always feed me, so there were days when I didn't eat much if anything at all. That, of course, kept me sick all the time, only she seldom took me to the doctor. Aunt Carla spent countless hours taking me back and forth to the doctor's office, getting me up to date on my vaccinations and working with a nutritionist to get me to a healthy weight. The two of them were by my side when I had my tonsils out, which was one reason I was always sick. Apparently, I was a strep carrier, and with the constant infections, my throat was always sore. I had a few complications, but she nursed me back to health."

"I do not like your mother," he emphatically states.

I grin. "Me either, now that I know that how she treated me is not the way you treat your own child. Anyhow, I eventually healed and started gaining weight. Once Aunt Carla was assured I would fit in at school and could hold my own, I was enrolled in the school here. I made a few friends but being alone so much when I was younger made it hard because I was almost painfully shy. Dax, you have to understand that I was punished whenever I spoke up, so I almost never talked."

He pulls me closer and kisses me gently before saying, "Continue, please. Although I have to say, this is difficult to listen to, but I know it was likely a lot worse than what you're saying."

Nodding, I say, "It was but my aunt and uncle loved me through it to the other side. Anyhow, I made a few friends, but they ended up moving away from here. So I went through middle school and then high school virtually alone. That's when I started focusing on my art. It was a way to escape the loneliness. Then, Uncle Jesse started letting me come to the shop with him and I found my career path."

"So, you had a shitty childhood until they rescued you. That still doesn't explain the look on your face when I told you that seeing the mark meant you were my mate."

Closing my eyes, I say, "This next part is hard for me." He pulls me closer so my head is on his chest, which gives me the courage to continue, "My senior year in high school, a boy that I had a secret crush on asked me to the prom. Oh, I was so excited! Aunt Carla and I went shopping for the perfect dress and the day of the prom, she took me to the salon, and they did my hair, makeup, and nails. I felt like a princess, Dax. My dress was so pretty, and Aunt Carla must've taken a hundred pictures that day while I was getting ready. My date arrived and Uncle Jesse gave him the standard 'dad' lecture about respecting me, etcetera, then we left. Dinner was wonderful; he took me to a steakhouse in the next town and then, we went to the prom."

The good memories of that night surface and I smile. The prom committee had transformed the banquet hall at the country club into a virtual paradise. Live plants and flowers decorated the room and twinkling lights gave it an almost ethereal feel. "It was magical, and I felt like I was on cloud nine. Finally, someone had noticed me, and we were getting along. I was already thinking about our next date, as well as my first kiss."

"What happened, sweetheart?" he whispers.

I can't help the tears that well up and slip down my cheeks. "Then it all went to hell. I was in a stall in the restroom when two girls came in, I guess to fix their makeup, but who knows? Anyhow, I overheard them saying that Trenton had won the first part of the bet."

"What bet?" The anger in his voice vibrates

throughout the room and I shiver, thinking about how he likely appeared all those years ago on the ship. Fierce, unyielding, protective.

"He-he had a bet with some of his friends that he could get me to go out with him, which he obviously won since I was there at the prom. It's the next part of the bet that he ended up losing though." Once again, my mind drifts back.

"Do you think he'll be able to do it?" Girl One asks. I don't recognize her voice since I tend to keep to myself, but I somehow know they're talking about me and Trenton, so I continue to listen.

"Don't see why not. Did you see how she's hanging onto every word he says? I almost feel sorry for him," Girl Two replies. Her voice sounds muffled, so I presume she's reapplying lipstick or lip gloss.

"Why? If you ask me, he's being an ass. I don't know her well, but she's pretty even if she's kind of quiet. And the dress she's wearing is gorgeous." I smile at that because Aunt Carla and I had a blast shopping for just the right dress.

"Because she seems like she's going to be a clinger. You know the only reason he took the bet is because he was

trying to make Jill jealous." I almost want to yell and ask about the second part of the bet, but I don't want them to know I'm in here, listening.

"Anyhow, Mark and Andrew got the rooms and they're going to be in the one next to him and Racine. When they think the time is right, they're going to sneak in through the connecting door and get pictures." Pictures? Of me and Trenton?

"Then what?" Girl One asks.

"Well, I think they plan to print them out and plaster the school with them, but Mark was also saying he might post them to social media."

"Jesus, that's harsh. What's she ever done to any of us?" Girl One states. I can hear the anger in her voice and wonder who she is that she's defending me like she is.

"It's just a joke," Girl Two defends.

"A joke that can have a lasting impact on her, don't you think?" Girl One questions.

"Maybe so, but I think it'd be funny," Girl Two replies. "You ready? I think the guys were sneaking something into the punch."

"Yeah," Girl One says. "I'm done here."

I wait long minutes to ensure they're gone before I call Aunt Carla. When she answers, I make an excuse about not feeling well and ask them to come and pick me up. Once I'm safe in their car, I send a text to Trenton to let him know I've gone home sick. I never hear from him again and he avoided me at school.

"Shhh, I've got you, baby. No one will ever hurt you like that again," he whispers in my ear, his hands running up and down my back. I can't bear to look at him right now, positive that he'll be disgusted by my stupidity.

"I never really dated again, Dax," I confess. Deciding to go for broke, I continue, "You were my first kiss."

"And I'll be your last kiss, sweetheart," he states. "So, what you're saying is you're an innocent."

I'm puzzled by the tone in his voice. He almost sounds...pleased. "Uh, yeah, that's what I'm saying. The witch couldn't have gotten it more wrong, Dax. I'm not very brave and still prefer my solitude to being around a lot of people."

He tilts my chin up until I'm forced to look him in the

eyes. "You have no idea how thrilled I am that I'll be your first, last, and only. But I plan to show you for the rest of our lives."

Another deep breath in, then out. Then again. Because what I'm about to say will likely upset him. I've heard the legend and know that the curse won't be fully broken until we have sex but I'm not ready to jump into bed with him yet. "Okay, spill it, baby. I can tell you've got something else on your mind." I nod but don't say anything. "You're safe to tell me anything, Racine."

"Maybe not this," I whisper.

He gives me a little shake and says, "*Anything*, Racine."

"I know how the curse gets broken, Dax, but I'm not ready for that yet," I admit.

His arms around me tighten slightly at my words, but instead of being angry, like I expect, he states, "I'm okay with going back as many months as it takes until you're ready, baby. Even though a part of me wishes you were, the fact of the matter is that this is going to be your first and only relationship. Can I ask one thing, though?"

"Yes," I reply.

"When I am here, can I stay with you so we can get to know one another better? And once we are mated, can we live here? Your home is so cozy and my cabin, which I know you've seen, is utilitarian at best."

"I'd like that," I softly say.

Dax

HEARING the hell that this precious woman went through has me so angry I want to hurt something or someone. And as much as I know I'd like to claim her fully this month, I was dead serious when I said we would wait as long as she needed. "How about we lock up and head to bed? I'd like to hold you tonight."

She glances up at me and I see her cheeks redden slightly. "Are you sure?"

"Yeah. Let's go check on Gizmo and then you go get ready while I lock up." She nods at me and climbs from my lap. It might not sound very warrior-like, but I already miss the feel of her in my arms.

I CHUCKLE when she comes out of the bathroom in a onesie that has paw prints all over it. "Cute, baby, real cute," I say as she slips into the bed.

"It's the height of fashion somewhere, I'm sure," she replies. I grin when she squeals as I tug her closer to me.

"I want you in my arms, Racine," I admit. "Plus, I want to kiss you some more."

"I-I think I'd like that," she says. Once again, her face flushes and I find myself looking forward to the day I can see just how far it goes down her luscious body.

WE SPEND the next two days together; talking, laughing, and kissing. As we walk toward the lake so I can go back, I hear her sniffle. I turn and pull her into my arms. "It's okay, Racine," I tell her. "This gives you the next month to think about all of it."

"I'll miss you, Dax," she replies, tears shimmering in her eyes.

"I'll be back before you know it, sweetheart. Now, kiss me and head home so I can shift and go back."

"See you next month," she murmurs as she leans up on her toes to kiss me. I pour everything into our kiss, knowing it'll have to last a month. I silently pray to my gods that when I return in December, she'll have made her decision.

CHAPTER 7

RACINE

One Month Later

I've spent the past month in a state of nervous anxiety, for lack of a better word. I reached out to Ailani, not wanting to discuss anything so...intimate...with Aunt Carla. She's been a godsend, increasing my knowledge so that I feel a lot better about being a virgin. Her last words to me were, "He knows you're an innocent, Racine. I promise that he'll make it good for you. And it will be good because a man like him won't settle for anything less."

Gizmo has a follow-up appointment today with Eric and I'm hoping that there's some improvement. He's gained a little weight back which is good, but I need to make sure that the prescription food is doing its job as well. Tonight's also the full moon and I know Dax will be showing up, so I hope he's onboard with what I've decided.

"Hey, Racine, how's he been doing?" Eric asks, coming into the exam room.

"Hey, Eric. He seems to have picked up a little weight," I reply. He nods and proceeds to weigh Gizmo then take the rest of his vitals.

"Feels like he's got a full bladder. Give me a few minutes and I'll see if we can get a urine specimen and check to see if he still has any crystals." I nod and sit down to wait, wishing I had Dax's arms to fall into again. True to his word, he didn't press the issue of sex last month, but I got used to sleeping in his arms those few nights and have been sleeping like crap ever since.

When Eric returns with Gizmo, I ask, "Well? Is it clear?"

"No, unfortunately. The good news is, we caught it early so with him on the special food, he should live a long life. I want to see him every three months to get a sample to make sure none of the crystals have gotten large enough to block off the opening and cause an infection. Of course, if at any time you have concerns, just call me."

"Thanks, Eric," I reply. "Oh! I almost forgot. This is for you," I say, handing him the check from the shop. When he gives me a puzzled look, I continue, saying, "Uncle Jesse and I have been running flash art specials every time we have a festival and we decided to donate the proceeds to you to use for the strays."

"I can't thank you enough, Racine. Ariel found a feral colony recently when she and Ailani were out walking and while they're not able to be adopted, I've trapped them, fixed them and released them back to where she found them. This will help us build some shelters for the winter months so they can stay warm and dry."

"We're going to keep doing it too, so hopefully it'll help," I reply.

"It's much appreciated," he says. "Okay, let's get you

scheduled for next month and then we'll go to every three months as long as things remain stable."

I'M STANDING at the water's edge waiting for Dax to emerge. The full moon shines bright and catches the twinkling lights that the town strung around the trees for some reason. I mean, I know it's Christmastime, but no one really comes down here. At least they're solar lights, so it isn't costing the town anything for electricity. It's cold out and there's about two feet of snow on the ground, so I brought a jacket I found in Dax's closet, as well as a pair of sweats and some boots. As I glance one more time at the water, I notice ripples that are steadily moving closer to the shore.

Dax

I'VE SPENT the last month replaying the three days I had with Racine. We spent a lot of time talking and my hope is that she'll have made her decision when I see her. She's sweet but has a feisty side, gets nervous whenever I touch her but eventually melts when I kiss her, and is everything my heart desires. As I step onto the shore, I see her standing there and smile. Then I notice how cold it is and wish, not for the first time, that I could put something at the water's edge that would hold clothes. She finally spots me and starts running toward me. Her teeth are chattering but she's holding out some clothes. "I brought you these," she says, finally reaching me. I notice that she's keeping her focus on my face and my grin widens. When I see the slight flush, I realize that she already looked and didn't miss the erection I'm sporting despite the cold water and even colder breeze that's blowing.

"Thanks, baby," I reply, quickly pulling the sweatpants on before I grab the sweatshirt and put it on. She then hands me my coat and a pair of socks, as well as my boots. "This is a first for me," I admit, once I'm fully dressed. I pull her into my side and kiss her. Not as long as I'd like, but she looks half-frozen, so I'll wait until we're somewhere warmer.

"What? Someone bringing you clothes? It's cold out, Dax!" she replies as I tuck her against my side and start walking toward her cottage. The closer we get, the more nervous she looks.

"What has you so freaked out, Racine?" I ask as we make it to her porch, and she unlocks the door.

"I-I-I, well, I hope you won't be mad," she says, her words coming out in a rush.

"About what?" I question as we walk through the door.

"About what I've done," she admits, taking off her hat, gloves, scarf, and coat and hanging them on the coatrack.

I glance around and start noticing things that weren't here last month. Specifically, my things. She's got my jackets on the coatrack, boots on the mat inside the front door, and if I'm not mistaken, a blanket that used to be in my cabin now rests on the back of her couch. Turning to her, I ask, "Does all of this mean what I think it does?"

Suddenly, my sweet little chatterbox, the woman who talks my ear off most of the time, becomes mute and won't look at me. "Racine? Honey, talk to me," I coax as I lead her to the couch. I get us situated then notice she has a tree up and decorated right in front of the window. "The tree looks beautiful, but isn't half as beautiful as you are."

"Dax, I spent this past month thinking about everything and I-I want to see what happens. I've never felt the attraction I feel with you toward anyone else in my life, so that must mean something, right? And because of that, I moved all of your things here. I hope that wasn't too presumptuous of me."

I lean my head back and laugh. Here I was worried that she would want to delay another month, maybe longer, and she has me moved in lock, stock, and barrel. "Oh, honey, no it wasn't. But are you sure? I mean, really sure? You know what happens once we make love. You'll get the same mark I have."

"I know." Her voice is quiet, almost whisper-like.

"You know you don't have to be scared of me, right?" I murmur against her ear. "Do you want me to tell you what my normal routine is the first night I come out of the water?" She nods so I say, "I go into my cabin, grab a beer and drink it, take a shower, then sleep for a few hours."

"I'll go grab you a beer," she states as she tries to get up. I hold onto her hips so she can't move and shake my head.

"Nuh-uh, sweetheart. First, I'm going to get my fill of you, then we'll do the rest of it, okay?"

"We?" she squeaks out.

"Yeah, baby, we," I reply. "Then after a nap, we'll see what we can get into, okay?" At her shy look and nod, I take my fill of her, reacquainting myself with her lips.

After long minutes, I stand with her in my arms and walk toward the kitchen where I grab us both drinks. She's holding onto me like a spider monkey, giggling, and I find myself joining her. When I see Gizmo winding himself through my legs, I ask, "Is he doing any better?"

"He is, yes, but I have to take him next month for a recheck. After that, if everything is good, then he'll go back every three months, unless I notice something going on."

I give her a quick kiss and state, "I'm glad, baby. I know how important he is to you." I've never had a pet, unless you count the countless fish that swim beneath the surface of Sapphire Lake, so her attachment to her cat is a bit foreign. I think I would be more of a dog person, myself, but I enjoy the antics of the little furball and if it makes my mate happy, then I'm happy.

Once I have our drinks secure, I walk toward her room where I deposit her onto the bed. She bounces a few times, causing her to giggle harder, and I find myself smiling. With the drinks now safe on the nightstand, I stalk toward her until I'm close enough. "Come on, Racine, time for our shower."

CHAPTER 8
RACINE

I feel jitters take over at the look he's giving me. There's lust, heat, and something I can't define right now. Placing my hand in his, he tugs me to an upright position, then leans down and kisses me. "I'm a bit nervous, Dax," I admit, waving my hand between us and then pointing at the bed. I know he knows this, but somehow, I feel the need to remind him that all of this is a first for me.

"You have no idea how happy that makes me, sweetheart," he states, picking me up so I'm cuddled close against him. I can feel the warmth emanating off him and realize that very soon, I'm going to be feeling him. My face flushes when I remember seeing how beautiful he looks naked. Wide shoulders, a smattering of chest hair, the darker hair that pointed to a massive erection. I'm a bit concerned that all of Ailani's good advice and suggestions won't work when I see how big he is, but until it happens, I'll go with the flow.

He sets me back on my feet then turns to start the shower and get the temperature just right. When he turns back toward me, I feel my panties combust at his look and I shiver. "Now what?" I whisper to myself.

"We get naked, get in the shower, clean up, then take a nap," he replies, reaching for the bottom of his sweatshirt. My mouth goes dry as he starts exposing more skin and I forget that I'm supposed to be undressing as well until he reaches for the hem at my waist. "Can't have you standing here ogling me," he teases once my shirt is over my head and tossed to the side.

"I was working on it!" I state. He grins at me and winks, letting me know I'm busted. "Really, I was, it's just that you're distracting me."

"Oh really," he drawls out, lowering his sweatpants. For my own sanity, I choose to keep looking at his face, causing him to chuckle. Once we're both completely naked, he takes me by the hand, and we step into the shower. "Here, let me," he says when I reach for my soap.

I sigh in contentment as he slowly but carefully washes me. Instead of making me nervous about what's to come, his touch comforts me while setting a small fire inside. He turns me so I'm under the spray then uses the hand-held sprayer and rinses me off. "I need to wash my hair," I confess when he moves me to the side. "It won't take long to dry, or I can put it in a braid." The gleam in his eyes tells me that I won't be styling my hair, at least not tonight.

Once my hair is clean and shiny, he again moves me then makes quick work of washing his own body. I keep stealing peeks at his impressive body as his large hands move efficiently to wash a month's worth of the lake off. He finally turns the water off and leads me out of the shower, then dries me carefully before wrapping me in a dry towel. He then dries himself and grabs my hairbrush. "Come on, baby, let's get your hair sorted so we can nap. I've been dreaming of having you in my arms since I left."

I'm nearly asleep when Dax finishes brushing my hair then braiding it. "How can you do that so quickly?" I murmur.

"Even though my hair is short now, I used to wear it long and sometimes, it got in the way, so I would braid it." I try to picture him with long hair and come up short since I've always known him with hair that is somewhat close-cropped.

"I can't imagine you with long hair," I tell him as he maneuvers us so that we're lying face-to-face.

"I'll gladly grow it out if you'd like," he replies. Kissing me quickly, he commands, "Now sleep, sweetheart. I've got plans for us when we wake up."

WAKING up ensconced in the warmth of his arms I realize a few things. The first is that somehow, he's now spooning me, his arm wrapped over my waist and the other over my head, as if even in sleep he's protecting me. The second is that something hard is pressing against my lower back and ass. Heat flushes my face when I realize up close and personal just how big he is. "Keep wiggling, Racine, and this will go a lot faster than it needs to given the circumstances." His voice rumbles low in my ear and I shiver with want and need.

"What if I want fast?" I muse.

He rolls me so that I'm flat on my back and props himself up on his elbow. "Not for this first time, sweetheart. Trust me on this, okay? Want to make it good for you."

I reach up to cup his jaw with my hand. "I trust you, Dax. Now, can you please make me yours?"

"With pleasure," he whispers, taking my mouth with his. Long, slow kisses coupled with his hand roaming lightly over my body soon has me writhing, wanting something I can't quite put into words. When his mouth lowers to capture a nipple, I feel myself growing wet with need. He moves back and forth, using his fingers to continue to tease the one he's not licking and sucking on, and all I can think is that this alone is driving me mad.

"Dax," I moan out. Thanks to Ailani, I now know more than the basics Aunt Carla gave me during our birds and bees discussion years ago, but she didn't tell me that there would be this...this almost combustible sensation growing inside!

"Shhh, I've got you, sweetheart," he murmurs before his hand dips between my thighs. "You're so responsive," he whispers as his fingers lightly stroke me. He hits what I know is my clit and I nearly come off the bed. Delicious, absolutely delicious and suddenly, I don't want to go slow any more.

"More, please," I whimper. I'm not sure what else I need, but something magnificent seems to be just out of my reach.

"I can see my mate is going to be demanding," he teases as he lowers himself. I feel him spreading my thighs and the blush I know is covering me spreads further. "Look at how wet you are," he says before leaning in and swiping his tongue from the bottom to my clit. Holy hell, does that feel good!

"God, Dax, that feels wonderful," I murmur. He does it again and again until I'm a writhing mess on the bed, my fists clutching at the sheets. When he adds a finger, I nearly detonate. "Fuck," I whisper. I had no clue that this could feel so damn good. Part of me is embarrassed at how I'm reacting, but another part simply doesn't care.

"You going to come on my tongue and fingers?" he asks.

"Maybe?" I have no clue, actually, because I've never had an orgasm, but if what I'm feeling is any indication, I may quickly become addicted to his touch.

"No maybe about it, baby," he replies, doubling his ministrations. The noises I'm now making should probably mortify me, but right now, I can't find it in me to care all that much because I'm flying higher and higher. I can feel my insides squeezing his fingers and realize that I'm about to experience a first, at least for me. When he lightly sucks on my clit, I let go, my back arching off the bed as I cry out his name. He continues licking and lightly thrusting his fingers until I begin to squirm as I'm now very sensitive. Chuckling, he stops then makes his way up my body, dropping open-mouth kisses on my flushed skin. He captures my lips with his and mimics his fingers' actions with his tongue which has my desire ramping up again.

I feel empty inside and realize I want him buried

within my heat. I press my hands to his hips in an effort to make him do something and he chuckles. "Patience, baby. Gotta go slow or it'll hurt you too much," he says. My whine has him kissing me again as he lines himself up at my opening. As he breaches me, I feel so many things at once that I nearly black out.

He feels like home, one that I never knew I wanted or needed.

He feels like forever, something I didn't anticipate ever happening.

He feels like a storm, all wild and free.

He feels like...mine.

Dax

I HISS in a breath as I work to enter her tight, wet heat. Nothing I've ever experienced before compares to this right now. She's so responsive and my heart soars at what that means for the two of us. I haven't even fully had her yet and I'm already planning the next time, and the time after that. Slowly, so slowly that I can feel sweat bead my forehead, I enter her an inch at a time. When I reach the undeniable proof of her innocence, I stop and lean my forehead against hers. "This is going to hurt, sweetheart." My heart aches that I'll be bringing her pain, even if it's brief, because what she's already given me has exceeded any expectations I ever had when it came to having a mate.

"Just do it, Dax. I trust you," she replies, looking up at me. "Besides, I'm sure you'll make it better."

I nod before taking a deep breath. When I think I'm ready, I kiss her in an effort to try and distract her from the upcoming discomfort. As she sighs, I push forward, breaking through. I keep going until I'm fully imbedded in her. She shudders and I stop. "You okay, baby?" I ask. As much as it would kill me, I'll stop right now if she says she's not.

A slight nod even as she avoids my eyes. "Look at me, Racine," I demand.

"I-I'm sorry I'm such a wuss and have no experience with this," she whispers, looking at me. I see the shimmer of tears in her eyes and wince, since the last thing I want to do is cause her pain.

"You're not a wuss and I'm not sorry. I'd beat my chest to show how pleased I am that you're only ever going to be mine, but I'm kind of busy right now," I reply. My body wants to move, to plunge into her over and over again until I find my release, but my mind and heart know that she needs time.

Her soft giggle as she reaches for my face has me smiling. "Dax? I think it's okay to move now."

I nod and slowly begin moving in and out of her body. As her desire ramps up, she grows wetter which eases my way. "You feel so fucking phenomenal," I grind out between clenched teeth. "Don't think this first time will last all that long," I admit. I can already feel my balls tightening, but I want this to be good for her as well.

"It doesn't matter, Dax," she replies.

"It does to me," I state, reaching between us to find her clit. I begin slowly rubbing it as I continue my thrusts and soon, I feel her legs encircle my hips. As my speed picks up, I notice her breathing has become erratic and I feel the flutters starting in her pussy. When she clamps down and keens out my name, I let myself go, plunging into her three more times before I detonate, filling her with my cum.

I continue moving inside her until her pussy has milked every drop out of me then drop to my side, pulling her with me so we're still connected. Kissing her deeply, I glance at her left bicep and see my mark now shimmering where once there was bare skin. "You're stuck with me now, mate," I growl out, possession and pride warring inside.

She sees where I'm looking and grins. "I guess I am. How soon can we do this again?" she asks, wiggling her hips and wresting a groan from me.

"I think we need to take it easy so you don't get sore," I say. I'm kind of clueless here simply because I've never been with an innocent. Most of my conquests have been with women who were experienced so our romps usually lasted well into the night. Somehow, I don't think Racine can handle that and now I wish I knew someone I could call.

"Well, that stinks," she says, causing me to laugh. "Wait, maybe I can Google it or something."

I raise my brow at her. "What's this Google?"

"Oh, it's a search engine on the computer. I'm sure there's something out there on the worldwide web that'll tell me what to do so I don't get sore. As soon as I can feel my legs again, I'll go get my phone and check!"

TRUE TO HER WORD, she looked up some things on her phone, so I find myself going into town to grab some Epsom salts for her to soak in. I grin as I walk into the store, eager to find what I'm looking for so I can get back to her. "Dax! Hey, Dax!" I turn and see my cousin and mentally groan. He teased me mercilessly while we were waiting for this month's full moon and I'm in too good of a mood to pound him into the ground.

I wait for him to get closer instead of bellowing back and when he does, I ask, "What are you doing here?"

"Shopping, same as you," he replies. I look at the basket he's carrying with suspicion because I suspect he saw me and followed me.

"What on earth could you need?" I question. His cabin, like mine, is fully stocked by his caretaker.

"Oh, you know, this and that," he says, following me. "You getting some flowers for your mate?" Flowers? Hell, I don't know if she even *likes* flowers! I close my eyes and picture her cottage and remember seeing flower beds that were prepared for the winter. Maybe I can grab her some. It's the thought that counts, right? I mean, I never courted a woman before I was cursed, too busy roaming the seven seas for what we could take.

"Why not?" I fire back, heading to the area of the store that I vaguely remember has flowers.

"Good. Women like that shit," he replies, grinning at me. "Get her some candy, too, I hear that works like a charm." I grimace because it appears he's going to give me a running commentary on anything I put in my cart and the minute he sees me put the Epsom salts and some lube in, he's going to make a smartass comment and then I'll be arrested by the sheriff for pounding him into the ground. I see it all happen so clearly that I don't notice him clearing his throat until he does it a few more times.

"You sick?" I ask. Not that it's happened since the curse; apparently, we no longer suffer those ailments, but who knows?

"No, man, was trying to get your attention," he says. "Now that you are back in the here and now, just wanted to say that I'm happy for you both. I know you were about to give up and stay in the lake so finding your mate has to be the best feeling in the world."

"It's unlike anything I ever expected or anticipated. Even talking with our former shipmates and hearing some of their stories didn't prepare me for the feelings that have grown so quickly when it comes to her," I state.

"I'm glad to hear it, Dax. Maybe there's still hope for me after all," he muses.

"Don't see why there isn't; I mean, if Jaxxen can find his mate, anyone can, right?" Jaxxen was one of us and had decided to never come out of the lake again until his brother told him he was getting married. He came topside and managed to find his mate, royally piss her off, then seal the deal anyhow.

"This is true. Anyhow, if it's not this month, it could be next, right?" he asks. "So, I've got to be ready." I chuckle as he waves his empty basket in the air.

"Whatever, Dayven. I've got shit to buy and no time to

chit-chat right now. Be sure you come visit next month."

"Fine, fine, I can take a hint. You take care of her, Dax. She seems pretty special."

"She is, she definitely is, Day."

CHAPTER 9
DAX

I walk back to the cottage, my arms laden with bags, grinning like a love-struck idiot. Not only did I find the items she asked for, I also grabbed her flowers, some chocolate, and a candle. The candle was the clerk's suggestion when she saw the rest of my items. She said that she always enjoys her bath surrounded by candles, not that I wanted the image of that in my brain! I also stopped by another store and I'm hoping that what I found there will make her happy. I hear a vehicle approaching behind me and I stop and turn. Seeing the sheriff's car, my eyebrow raises. When he lowers the passenger window, I ask, "Everything okay, Sheriff?" He's a nice man, has been here for as long as I remember and takes the monthly ebb and flow of all of us descending on Aurora Falls with a grain of salt.

"Saw you walking and figured I'd give you a ride," he says. "Hop in."

I don't question his offer because it's fucking cold out and the bags are bulky enough that I can't move as fast as I'd like. "Appreciate it," I say, putting the bags in the back before getting into the passenger seat. "Didn't know you could do stuff like this."

"Why not? It's my town, I'm the sheriff, so if I see one of my people walking, as long as I've got nobody in the back, I should be able to give them a ride, right?"

"I don't see why not."

"Plus, I'm on patrol and going the same way, so it's not like I'm wasting gas or anything," he says, putting the squad car in gear.

"This is true," I reply.

"So, you and Racine, huh?" he inquires.

"News travels fast, I see." I'm not surprised. The lake people are a well-kept secret that most know about. It's only the tourists who are really kept in the dark.

"She's a sweet girl. Life could have been a lot worse for her if Jesse and Carla hadn't stepped in and brought her home to Aurora Falls."

I feel my anger rise at what I know of her mother. "If I ever meet that woman and she's on fire, I will not put her out," I declare. "She broke that little girl's spirit and to this day, even though she's a strong, independent woman, I've seen glimpses of that little girl that kill me."

The sheriff nods at my words. "I think there would be a bunch of us who would watch that. If you could have seen her then, Dax. She was this tiny little thing, scared of her own shadow, afraid to talk. It broke my heart. Then, seeing her come out of her shell the longer she was with Jesse and Carla was almost miraculous. She was always shy, though, and after something happened at prom, she pretty much kept to herself."

Speaking of which...I hold my hand up and ask, "Do you know this Trenton character? It seems he needs a lesson in manners." Maybe I can work out some aggression on him; he sure as hell deserves it.

Sheriff Holmes gives me a knowing look before saying, "As much as I agree with you, he can't hurt her anymore, not where he's at."

"And where's that?" I don't have a job yet so while she's working, I can seek him out and make sure he knows that how he treated her was not right.

"Over there," he replies, pointing toward the right. I glance over in time to see the sign for the Aurora Falls Cemetery.

Okay, I didn't want him dead. Or did I? If she hadn't found out what his plans were, she would have been humiliated and I simply can't let that stand. "What happened?" I ask as curiosity finally overwhelms my desire to destroy him.

"Seems he was carrying on with someone else and his wife, Jill, found out. It wasn't the first time, but this time, he got his mistress pregnant and was planning to leave his wife or something like that. She snapped and shot him dead one night when he came in after spending a night with his mistress."

"Where is she now? His wife, that is." No clue why I feel sorry for her, except that this cretin of a man managed to dupe her.

"Well, originally, she was charged with his murder until all the details came out. Then, it was downgraded to manslaughter with the caveat that she had temporarily lost her mind. She spent a few years in a local sanitarium and is now living a few towns over. The mistress ended up not being pregnant and when she found out he was married, because he told her they were going through a divorce, she moved away as well."

"Good. Racine doesn't need those reminders around here," I emphatically state.

"No, she doesn't. Still a tragedy, though, that one man destroyed so many lives."

As he pulls into the driveway, I see the twinkling lights in the window and smile. "I'm going to need to find a job now that I'm a permanent resident in Aurora Falls. Know of anything in town?"

He nods and says, "It's not much to start, but we're looking for some help down at the station. I think your size alone would give you an advantage because no one will mess with you."

"What is it?"

"I need a jailer, someone who can keep an eye on anyone we lock up," he advises, putting the car in park.

"I can do that, I'm sure," I advise.

"Good, then come see me after the holidays. That'll be soon enough to join the work force," he says, giving me a grin.

"I'll be there," I promise, getting out of the car and grabbing my bags from the back. Giving him a wave, I walk up to the porch and am about to open the door when it opens from the inside and I see my woman, my mate standing there. "Hey, baby," I murmur, leaning down to kiss her lips. They're still plump from all the kissing we did earlier, and I make a mental note to see just how swollen I can make them.

"Hey, yourself," she replies, before trying to grab the bags.

"Nope, I've got them, you lock up," I command as I stride into the kitchen. By the time she comes in, I've got the flowers out and in a vase that I found under the sink.

"Oh, Dax, they're beautiful!" she cries, coming over to me. "Thank you so much!"

I grin down at her; her enthusiasm about such a small thing has me pulling her close and kissing her until we're both breathless. Finally stepping back, I gruffly state, "Got the other stuff, too." I see her face redden and grin. "Come on, sweetheart. I've got plans for the two of us and the first one involves you soaking in a tub so that we prevent you getting too sore."

"Dax! You can't say that!" Her face is even redder, and I throw my head back and laugh.

"I most certainly can, and I have a lot more you'll be hearing later," I tease, wiggling my eyes at her. It's time for my shy maiden to know how this Viking really can be. I scoop her up and grab the bag with the other items and head back to the bedroom. School is now in session!

Racine

I BLINK AT HIM, unable to form words just yet. "Are you okay?" he asks, his worried look finally unfreezing my vocal cords.

"I-I had no idea. I mean, the first time was like, wow. But this time surpassed anything I ever imagined," I admit. True to his word, we had bathed in the Epsom salts, then he had carried me to bed. The first time, he had said it was all about me as he used his lips, tongue, and fingers to send me into oblivion. But the next time, after a brief nap where he cuddled me close, he made me be on top. I Ioly hell, I felt like a wanton woman as I let the feelings take me over until my hair was whipping around my head.

"I suspect it will get better the longer we're together," he says, his voice husky from yelling my name.

"I think you're right."

"Do you want to go into town?" he asks. "I'd like to see it all lit up at night."

"I'd like that. We'll have to dress warm, though, because the temperature was supposed to start dropping again. I think the forecast is calling for snow," I reply.

"We can do that, especially since you brought all my stuff over here." I blush because I did do that, even going so far as to get a matching dresser for his things. "Now, baby, why are you blushing?"

"Because it was a bit bold of me to do that, don't you think?" I question.

"Why? You're my mate. Who else is supposed to take care of me if not you?"

"Well, when you put it that way, I guess you're right," I admit. "Okay, if we're going to do that, let's get ready."

He laughs and gets out of the bed, stopping my breath again. He's a work of art and I pinch myself to make sure that it's real, not just some delusional fantasy I've dreamed up. "You getting up or are you going to keep looking at me like I'm a meal and you're the starving woman."

His comment makes me laugh as I crawl out of the bed. Just like I normally do, I start making it. "What are you doing?" he asks.

"Making the bed, of course," I reply.

"But why? We're just going to crawl back into it when we get back home," he questions.

"Just another of those weird quirks of mine, Dax," I say. "Until Uncle Jesse came and got me, I had a mattress and a blanket. When I moved in with them, Aunt Carla took me shopping for decorations and I vowed then to always make my bed." He nods and starts helping me make the bed without saying another word. Once we're done, I head to the closet to grab some clothes, then walk into the bathroom to get ready.

Ten minutes later, I'm as together as I'll ever get so I leave the bathroom and search out Gizmo. When I get to the living room and see him in the window next to the tree, the twinkling lights causing his fur to sparkle, I start laughing. "You're a silly boy, aren't you?" I ask as I pick him up and walk to the kitchen.

"I was just fixing his food," Dax says. "I hope I did it correctly."

"He gets one can of the wet food three times a day," I advise, putting Gizmo down in front of the bowl. "So as long as you put a full can in his bowl, you did it right."

"Good. You ready?" he asks.

"Just have to get my coat on. Are we driving or walking?" I see his grimace and grin because I did something else this past month that he doesn't know about. "Never mind, we're driving. It's going to be cold enough walking around so why start out the night frozen?" I walk to the closet and pull our jackets down then smile when he takes mine from me and helps me put it on. He may think he's a rough and rugged Viking, but when it comes to me, he's attentive and caring.

Once he wraps my scarf around my neck, he uses the ends to draw me closer, then leans down and kisses my nose. "I guess I can suffer riding in the clown mobile so that you stay warm."

I smirk as I snag my purse and keys and head toward the garage. "You'll be fine," I tell him as we walk into the enclosed space and I unlock my new Jeep. I see his eyes widen when he notices the new vehicle.

"You bought another car?"

"Yes. Once I realized that I wanted to see where all of this went, I knew I had to get something bigger. I went to ask Uncle Jesse to go with me and help and he and

Aunt Carla surprised me with this, saying it was from my grandfather's estate."

"That was nice of them," he says, walking to the driver's side and opening the door for me.

"I know! I was beyond shocked, but Uncle Jesse said that my grandpa, knowing how my mother was, put my inheritance into a trust with him, Uncle Jesse that is, as the trustee. So, he helped me buy a new car. Do you like it?" I ask as he gets in on the passenger side.

"It's a lot more comfortable than your old one, that's for sure," he teases as he puts his seatbelt on.

I start it up after opening the garage door, then carefully back out. "It's got a rearview camera thingy too, see?" I state, pointing at the screen.

"That's cool. What else does it have?" he asks.

"Well, hands-free calling, a navigation system, heated seats, some really cool radio system that I downloaded onto my phone since I never really go anywhere but to work and home, those kinds of things," I reply.

"Wait, heated seats?"

"Yep." I push the buttons and say, "Give it a minute or so and you'll be nice and toasty."

As we drive into town, I point out the different cottages that have light displays. I've always enjoyed Christmas, even before I went to live with Uncle Jesse and Aunt Carla. There's a magic in the air and people are just more friendly. "You weren't kidding about the seats," he says, breaking into my silent reverie.

"Oh! And it has a remote starter which is nice at the end of the day."

"What does that mean?" he questions.

"I can use my car keys to start my car from inside the shop."

"Won't it get stolen?"

"No, it stays locked until I get to it, but as long as I remember to keep the heat on, it heats the inside so when I do get outside to it, I don't freeze for half my trip," I reply.

"Makes sense." I nod as I park the Jeep along Main Street. "We're walking from here?"

"We are, but I thought we'd grab a hot cocoa from over

there first," I say, pointing to my favorite vendor in the winter.

"I guess you do like chocolate," he murmurs.

"Absolutely. Especially at certain times of the month," I blurt out, then when I realize what I've said, I cover my mouth as he bursts out laughing.

"I'll keep that in mind, sweetheart. Now, come on, we've got stuff to see and do," he states, grabbing my hand in his and pulling me into the warmth of his body. "First stop, hot cocoa for my mate," he whispers, so low I'm the only one who hears him.

The next hour or so is spent checking out the festival vendors who are willing to brave the cold for the shoppers. I find a few more gifts and soon, Dax has a bag slung over his shoulder. When we finally get to the town Christmas tree, I stop and stare in awe. Every year, the town's committee seems to find the perfect tree and then decorates it to showcase not only our town's heritage, but also the quaint, homey feel that resonates through our mountains. This year, they've hung blue and light green lights, and the ornaments are a mix of giant sparkling balls and baubles. "It's beautiful," I whisper, looking up.

"Not half as beautiful as you," he whispers in my ear. When I glance up at him, it's to see him now kneeling in front of me.

"Dax? What are you doing?" I ask.

"Asking you to marry me. Well, trying to," he replies. I notice a small crowd has gathered and am shocked when I see Uncle Jesse and Aunt Carla standing there, him grinning ear to ear and her with her phone up and videoing what is happening. When I don't respond, he clears his throat and takes my hand in his. "Knowing that you were destined to be mine, long before you came into existence is a bit disconcerting, but in our short time together, I've grown to love you, Racine. I want all of your days to be by my side; the good, the bad, the happy, the sad. Please say you'll marry me?"

I can barely see him through the tears streaming down my face, so I nod before saying, "Yes, Dax, I'll marry you." He places a gorgeous ring on my finger then stands, picking me up and twirling me. I stroke his cheek and whisper, "Because I love you too, Dax."

As he kisses me, I vaguely hear the cheers from my family and the friends I've made. Despite living here most of my life, I'm finally home.

One Year Later
Racine

I grin as I wrap another gift, gently swatting Gizmo's paws away yet again. He's held his own this past year and at the last visit, Eric said that the crystals were almost non-existent. Everything that's happened since Dax asked me to marry him has been nothing short of miraculous. We decided to get married by the Justice of Peace that Uncle Jesse said owed him a few favors instead of waiting. Getting married underneath the lights at the Christmas tree in town on Christmas Eve is one of my favorite memories. Uncle Jesse gave me two weeks off and we stayed holed up at home the first week, learning about each other. I honestly had no clue there were so many ways a couple could have sex, but I know now, that's for sure. I pat my baby bump and smile, remembering how excited Dax was the first time we heard the heartbeat and saw our tiny peanut on the sonogram machine.

The most unexpected thing of all, however, is that Dax's cousin met his mate. Surprisingly, it was at the St. Patrick's festival. She was a vendor and had poured him a beer and when he took it, someone jostled him and she ended up spilling it all over him. When he raised his shirt, she saw his mark on his lower abdomen. He teases Dax all the time that his love of a 'good ale' is what brought his mate to him. Regardless, they're happy and planning a huge wedding for New Year's Eve.

"You're not done yet?" Dax asks, walking into our room. He's in his uniform as the town jailer and I try not to drool at how awesome he looks, but I'm afraid that may be impossible thanks to the hormones that are running rampant in my body.

"Just about," I reply. "I need to get up though. I think our son is on my bladder." He laughs as he hauls me up and puts me on my feet. I waddle as fast as I can into the bathroom, giggling at how funny I must look.

Once I'm done and have washed my hands, I walk back into our room and smile. He's changed into a pair of plaid lounge pants and a white t-shirt and is now sprawled on the bed. He motions to me so I crawl up alongside him then let out a shriek as he pulls me so my head is on his chest. "What are you doing? I've got more stuff to wrap!"

"We're taking a nap, my beloved wife. Just toss the rest of the stuff into those bags you bought." The man likes his naps, that's for damn sure! He pulls the throw at the end of the bed up until we're both covered, then claps his hands so the lights go out. I bought it as a gag last year, but he loves it because we can have the lights on until we're both in bed. Wait until he sees what I got for him this year, one that's voice activated!

"Oh we are, are we?" I tease as his hands roam over my

body. My libido has been off the chain since finding out I was pregnant and at just a touch from him, I'm ready to go.

"Yes, we are. Then, I plan to make love to you all night long to celebrate."

I frown because our anniversary is still a week away. "What did I forget?"

"The first time, sweetheart, that you gave yourself to me. Out of all the times we've made love, that is one of my most treasured memories."

Oh, he's a smooth talker, my husband! "All of them are mine, Dax," I admit. No matter how many times he reaches for me or I reach for him, it's always spectacular.

"Well, you dream of them and when we wake up, I'll make all your dreams come true," he promises, placing a kiss on my forehead.

"You already have," I whisper. "You already have."

The End

I hope you enjoyed your trip to Aurora Falls! Check out the rest of the stories in the series and fall in love with the other authors' characters!

DARLENE'S FOLLOW LINKS

Facebook Author Page:

https://www.facebook.com/darlenetallmanauthor/

Darlene's Dolls Group Page:

https://www.facebook.com/
groups/1024089434417791/

Rebel Guardians Insiders:

https://www.facebook.com/
groups/280929722515781/

Newsletter Subscriber Link:

http://eepurl.com/dEaxGj

Amazon Author Page:

https://www.amazon.com/Darlene-
Tallman/e/B01LC3YKAY/

Goodreads:

https://www.goodreads.com/author/show/15709175.Darlene_Tallman

Bookbub:

https://www.bookbub.com/authors/darlene-tallman

ABOUT DARLENE

I'm a lifelong reader who had a dream to write her own books. A transplanted Yankee, I recently moved cross country from Georgia to Texas. While I have a strong personal belief system and faith, I won't be "preaching" in any of my books. They'll have perfectly imperfect people in it who meet, fall in love, fall into bed (at times; sometimes they might wait), have kids, get married. In short, I want to write books that make people think and feel.

My debut novel, "Bountiful Harvest" was released on the 7th anniversary of my mom's death. Somehow, I think my biggest cheerleader and staunchest defender helped it publish so quickly.

Since hitting publish 8/31/16, I've had the privilege to begin co-writing with Liberty Parker on an MC series, the Rebel Guardians. There are seven books out in this series, plus two books in a spin-off (2.0, the next generation) and the first book in The Nelson Brothers (who show up in book 5 of the RGMC). We're hard at work on yet another spin-off (New Beginnings) featuring some of the girls from the RGMC whose love interests are not with the men from the MC!

I also co-write a series of children's short stories with a fellow author, Cherry Shephard and her 10 year old son. Get immersed in "The Mischief Kitties" and their zany, crazy lives!

The Mischief Kitties in the Great Glitter Caper

The Mischief Kitties in You Can't Takes Our Chicken

The Black Tuxedos MC

1. The Black Tuxedos MC - Reese

2. Nick - The Black Tuxedos MC

Rebel Guardians MC (with Liberty Parker)

Braxton

Hatchet

Chief

Smokey & Bandit

Law

Capone

A Twisted Kind Of Love

Rebel Guardians Next Generation (with Liberty Parker)

1. Talon & Claree

2. Jaxson & Ralynn

New Beginnings (with Liberty Parker)

1. Reclaiming Maysen

2. Reviving Luca

Nelson Brothers (with Liberty Parker)

1. Seeking Our Revenge

2. Seeking Our Forever

Old Ladies Club (with Kayce Kyle, Erin Osborne and Liberty Parker)

1. Old Ladies Club - Wild Kings MC

2. The Old Ladies Club - Soul Shifterz MC

3. Old Ladies Club - Rebel Guardians MC

4. Old Ladies Club - Rage Ryders MC

With Various Other Authors

Poetry: Dreams You Catch

www.ingramcontent.com/pod-product-compliance
Lightning Source LLC
Chambersburg PA
CBHW071956150726
47999CB00001B/457